# Books by Geoffrey Household

# THE
# SENDING

# THE
# SENDING

GEOFFREY HOUSEHOLD

*An Atlantic Monthly Press Book*
LITTLE, BROWN AND COMPANY · BOSTON · TORONTO

FIRST AMERICAN EDITION

Library of Congress Cataloging in Publication Data

Household, Geoffrey, 1900–
  The sending.

  "An Atlantic Monthly Press book."
  I. Title.
  PZ3.H8159Se  1980  [PR6015.07885]  823'.9'12  79-24664
  ISBN 0-316-37438-5

ATLANTIC—LITTLE, BROWN BOOKS
ARE PUBLISHED BY
LITTLE, BROWN AND COMPANY
IN ASSOCIATION WITH
THE ATLANTIC MONTHLY PRESS

BP

Designed by D. Christine Benders

*Published simultaneously in Canada
by Little, Brown & Company (Canada) Limited*

PRINTED IN THE UNITED STATES OF AMERICA

# THE
# SENDING

# I

## June 2

I am being followed. I do not know by whom or what.

It cannot be nothing. I cannot convince myself that it is imagination. I look back. Never in my life have I suffered from paranoia or a persecution complex or whatever name a psychiatrist would give to this delusion. Meg registers that I am not ill, and she is not afraid. That means nothing. She is by nature fearless. She would stand on her hind legs and chatter at a lion, and the lion, I think, would find business elsewhere.

It is not a delusion. Could a delusion make me run, run

with a few necessaries from a house I love and trust, leaving behind a feebly lying note? Behind every door it was waiting for me. What was waiting for me? Nothing! But no house is safe. Houses have walls; one cannot see what is in the next room. That is why I have taken to the open. I can see around me.

Then why am I not more afraid at night? I am not. Day and night I am steadily afraid. I do not know any malaise in my life with which I can compare this incubus. Indigestion perhaps, with its continual weight of which one is conscious. But that is merely discomfort. The weight of fear is different.

Fear of what? Not of death. The fear of death is healthy, natural, easily to be overcome by faith or courage or loyalty. An animal, I presume, has no conception of death. When threatened it runs. The genes, passionate for survival, make it run. That is what I am like: a doomed animal running. Being a man, I want to know why. Yet all I can tell is that the threat is to my mind, my very conscious self, not — or not directly — to my body. But obviously if this goes on much longer the destruction of the personality must lead to destruction of the body in the end.

That is why I am writing: to save what can be saved. The analysis forced by written words should be as effective as answering the questions of a psychiatrist. One is compelled to make sense of the unintelligible if only to oneself. Already I see that I cannot be other than sane. Only a sane man would stop at a village shop and buy a notebook in which to record his insanity.

I am thirty miles from home, on the Purbeck Hills. I am one with my land. Under my body is short grass and thyme, and beneath me is an ancestor — for I am resting on a tumulus of the dead — who loved as I do. I am

4

alone with the wind and yet within sight, as in a dreamed landscape, are all the activities of man. To the northeast is Poole Harbour, a setting of deep browns and greens for the uncut diamond of the water flecked with white sails of yachts. To the west is mile after mile of farmland and village; and beyond, cut off from sight by the waves of downland, are the valleys of gray and emerald, fine timber and churches and water meadows which I cannot see but know are there, like the smile behind the eyes of a beloved woman. To the south is the sea, the emptiness of the sea from the Needles to Portland Bill, the blue, happy surface where there is no mystery, and beneath it only peace.

I don't like this place. I have been followed here.

All right, all right! So you were followed. What by? The singing of the larks? Now are you more satisfied, tucked away in the cover of this hanger beneath the northern slopes after running again for your life, this time emptying bowels and bladder and quite unaware of it till you crouched down? It's going to take time to find you, isn't it? You bloody fool, do you think you are a rabbit? And didn't you write, when you were up there in the open, that the fear was not of death?

Agoraphobia. Only at ease in a closed place or with a companion. Well, I refuse any companion except Meg. The unknown would not go away. I know that. The last time I called on Rita — hope of comfort? — I was continually looking over my shoulder and I thanked heaven that she was a woman and went first through doors. No, no companion for me in my present state! I am unfit for a companion. So it is not agoraphobia but some other form of mild insanity.

To be attacked through the receptors of one's brain is

5

for self-conscious man worse than any bodily attack. For an animal it is no more than the wordless recognition that it had better run or freeze. Or fight? But that is rare in nature, unless against man or for a mate. Yet it is what I should do — fight! Perhaps I am fighting already. Perhaps the mere buying of this notebook is the declaration of war.

But fight what? Well, I am safe in cover, watched but not closely. I will go back over my recent life. Paddy's death three weeks ago — could it be Paddy's death which is affecting me? It was my car that killed him, but as I was not in it at the time I could hardly feel guilt even subconsciously.

No, it's not that. Remembering Paddy calms me. Whatever is stalking me, whether inside me or outside, does not like thoughts of Paddy, so I will write about him. Go away! I am not here. I am in the past.

He was a saddler and a devoted craftsman, known throughout the county. Considered as a plain tradesman, he was exasperating, for you could never be sure of finding him in his shop. When you did find him you wouldn't get out under half an hour. Meanwhile he would work on whatever you had brought in to be mended or help you to define what you needed by making a rough drawing of it. It was often best to be last in the line for his services. The latest job was done immediately while less urgent leatherwork might hang about in the shop for months.

That was because he was so often away. Over the forty years of his working life he had built up a reputation among horsemen for more than bridles and saddles. I imagine it could have started while he measured some temperamental two-year-old and the horse was calm and interested as any man at a fashionable tailor. However that may be, the word went around among a small,

6

knowledgeable circle — had even gone across the Channel — that Paddy was a genius with problem horses of superb breeding but little value. Whether the difficulties were minor but exhausting of patience, such as ungovernable refusal to be clipped, rasped or shoed, or whether they were fundamental failures in breaking or training, Paddy might be asked to try his hand or give his advice. Close at home he would spend hours on a child's pony and charge nothing. For more distant or more celebrated customers he had, I believe, no fixed fee; they could make out the check for whatever they liked. And they must have liked. He was very comfortably off for a saddler in a small country town.

He was the most Christian character I have ever met, if one can call him so when he never went to church and had no apparent interest in religion. He assumed everyone to be as full of benevolence as himself without asking what laws, beliefs or upbringing made them so, and took altruism as the natural state of any animal, including man. In his presence that seemed to be true, and the aura was pervasive. He was known to be careless with money and his shop was easy to break into from the quiet lane behind, but nobody ever tried it. We had a fair quota of juvenile delinquents always on the lookout for anything that could be stolen without much risk, yet they left Paddy alone. Perhaps they thought there must be a catch in it somewhere or perhaps they were afraid of Meg.

Meg is a wild polecat, about a foot long not counting the tail, her color blending with the dark woodland earth when out for blood, handsomely black when at ease. Paddy told me that he had picked her up in Wales, only survivor of a litter which had been disgracefully but justifiably exterminated by an angry pony-breeder who was also a turkey farmer. Thereafter the pair were inseparable. He

7

took Meg for walks occasionally to keep her fit and give her the satisfaction of killing a rabbit, but the polecat's usual place was in the workshop or in a large inner pocket of Paddy's coat. She must have been the runt of the litter, for she is still small for her breed. She never attempted to escape. Acquired characteristics had largely overcome instinct. Paddy was the only parent she knew and a Divine Polecat; what It did must be right.

I never heard of her attacking anyone, but it could be disconcerting suddenly to see movement as an apparent parcel of black saddle-stuffing uncoiled and humped itself across the floor of the workshop like a giant, furry caterpillar. Paddy always encouraged me to handle and play with her. When he was away on one of his journeys he would give me the key to the workshop and ask me to drop in with Meg's breakfast and supper. Chopped heart or kidney it was. No nonsense of the bread-and-milk of ferret feeding. Paddy wanted the full sensitivity of an out-and-out carnivore. So Meg came to accept me as the chosen priest of her god. I got a gentle nip from her once in a while if she was out of temper or indeed if I was. She has always been uncannily responsive to mood.

Paddy's will left everything to some niece of his with the exception of small bequests to friends. I found that he had left me Meg. Or not quite that. He was too courteous to put anyone under an obligation which might be unwelcome. He had merely requested me to look after Meg if I wasn't disinclined. Like all the Mustelidae she is highly intelligent and outrageously playful. A favorite sport is hide-and-seek. She chatters with pretended fury when caught, striking like a snake at the hand held out to her without ever drawing blood. She will then climb ecstatically onto my head, prospecting for more amusement in middle earth. I know I cannot communicate with her as

8

Paddy did, but she is gradually teaching me much more than her games.

Paddy himself had the profound, inborn understanding of animals which primitive man has never lost. He never forgot that he too was an animal, so that his remarks were always revealing. To explain motives and behavior he looked inside himself rather than to detailed study followed by conjecture. He resembled my blood brother of the forest who taught me years ago to attempt unity with any living creature — to think as it might, to feel as it does, to mimic its movement.

Yes, it helps to remember Paddy and the past and further back into the past, so it may be good for me to form a picture of myself — or what was myself — from the outside. Seldom ill, thank God, and as fit as ever I was. Retired from the Indian Army. That description makes me, I know, a creature of inscrutable past and causes puzzled stares since it implies that I must be in my seventies while I am only in the early forties. It was not of course the imperial Indian Army but the present army. National Service as a sapper led me into cartography. Volunteered for Malaya because mountains were more fun to map than Salisbury Plain. Indian government was seeking qualified surveyors and cartographers, and I was accepted. Liked the country. Was invited to stay on. Finished up as an official cartographer at GHQ, which inevitably gave me the rank of colonel. The officers I trained appear to have been fond of me; what is certain is that I was fond of them. Perhaps they took the place of the sons I might have had if my wife had not died so young and in my arms.

I returned permanently to England after my father's death. The decision was not easy. But I am the last of a very long line and the call of the country and county and home of my ancestors was too strong. To be afraid of that house, how insane!

I must try to avoid that word. Words have authority.

Have I any guilt at selling off the land? I see no reason why I should have. I am not a farmer. Perhaps I could have been, starting early enough, since I am not content unless I am creating something; but creation to me is a thing of the mind, not hard, physical labor, which is fine as relaxation but deadens sensitivity. It's odd how a snatch of conversation can suddenly reveal or exemplify a truth. One of my neighbors, coming upon me when I was terracing and manuring a bank for vines said: "Always working, I see." I replied without a thought: "No, I am idling."

I wanted, have always wanted to paint. As a boy I was well taught and had a hobby for life. And so when I came home I took to it as a profession, keeping the house of my ancestors, the parkland and the wood across the valley, but leasing the grazing and selling all the outlying parts of the estate. Today I am near to living by my art; but the decision to give myself freedom to develop without bothering whether I sold my work or not was, I am sure, right.

As a painter I belong to no school and shall never be among the great. I am a translator. It is my business to make other eyes see what my own eyes see — in fact to translate my joy and the mystery of it. Often, I know, I fall into mere prettiness; but sometimes on a great day when light and nature combine into a unity appreciable by every living thing within the landscape, then the result, I am told, is curiously haunting and unforgettable.

Can it be that which haunts me — a personification of my own occasional power? I do not think so. I should surrender to it. I should not be deadly afraid.

10

And I have tried to be of use. It is perfectly possible to accept two clear disciplines: one of the craft and one of the society accepted by my ancestors. I have the simplicity of a dutiful and happy dog. I cannot detect in that self anything out of the ordinary, anything abnormal. "Men like Alfgif Hollaston are the backbone of the English countryside," said some pompous chairman introducing me. Is he? Well, he's got a slipped disc in these days.

That's better, old son! I don't think it likes humor.

Giving it personality, are you? Crazier than ever! But that may be the right way of looking at it. A person can be fought. I can still keep an open mind. That's one of my few virtues I am sure of. I am full of curiosity, as full as Meg. I rule out nothing and judge a theory — religion, for example — on its merits. Does it give results or doesn't it?

Paddy's death. I return to that. The police have never found out the cause of it, and I am no nearer a solution than at the time. In these days my curiosity is more occupied by his Meg, who suggests so many answers to questions but, like a computer, is limited to yes or no.

Paddy was killed on the night of May 12 while walking along the Pidge: a narrow, winding lane forming a long loop off the main road and returning to it. It serves only two farms, one at each end, so the middle is pretty well deserted except by pedestrians out for a quiet country walk and riders on the wide grass shoulders. I cannot begin to guess what Paddy was doing on the Pidge after dark and on foot. A night spent in communion with animal life is likely. Badgers? Bats? Moths? Or had he been out there earlier in the day and was searching for something he had lost from his pocket?

He was found next morning in the middle of the lane. He had been struck by a passing car, run over and killed

11

instantly. The driver might have had his lights out, but even so in the utter silence Paddy must have heard the car and could easily have moved out of the way onto the grass shoulder.

It was an obvious case of manslaughter and a possible case of murder. A tenable theory was that Paddy had set out to a secret meeting on the Pidge — a perfect spot for it — and had been deliberately assassinated. Loved though he was by everyone in Penminster, he could well have made some enemies elsewhere in the jealous horsy world; but police, after inquiries among his friends and customers, were strongly against anything of the sort. However inexplicable the accident, a local man familiar with the Pidge and using it for some illegal purpose was probably involved.

And then the wildest bit of good luck or bad luck, according to how one looks at it! For a couple of days before Paddy's death I had been running with a spare on the left front wheel. It happened to be an old but hardly used radial tire with a distinctive tread unlike the other three. When I drove into the Penminster garage where they had been mending the puncture on my regular tire, the proprietor said to me with some embarrassment that he was very sorry but he had been asked to report to the police immediately if any car came in with three well-used tires and one new radial. Of course I had no objection and went off to lunch at the Royal George. When I returned a police van was in the garage courtyard, with three experts around my car. They told me at once that my car had killed Mr. Gadsden, cautioned me and asked if I would care to make a statement. Behind the bumper they had found a trace of blood and a shred of cloth which matched Paddy's trousers. In the tread of a tire was imbedded one of Paddy's teeth. There was no doubt that it was my car which had struck Paddy and that the right rear wheel had crushed his jaw and neck.

I had no trouble in clearing myself. On the night of Paddy's death I had been at the housewarming party given by Sir Victor Pirrone. The Manor House is on the edge of our little town and hardly more than a mile from my home, so I walked. That is considered eccentric, but I always do if I am likely to be lavishly entertained in Penminster. I reckon that I shall not be in a fit state to drive when I leave, though sober enough to enjoy the walk home grateful for life and with heightened perception. There is the added advantage that I can leave when I choose without waiting for a lift — a lift which is bound to be inconvenient since my house is on the way to nowhere and approached from the main road by a farm track which my father refused to surface in order to prevent, as he said, fools turning down it in the hope that it led to the valley below.

My presence at the Pirrones from eight to two was confirmed by Rita Vernon and one of our local magistrates as well as by the High Sheriff. I had even been accompanied for part of the way home by Police Constable Warrender wheeling his bicycle who was taking a shortcut to investigate a rick fire. He was able to state that when he passed the house my car was standing outside the front door where I had left it. Neither of us had any reason to examine it closely.

So there was no doubt that my car had been stolen and that the culprit had audaciously put it back exactly where it had been instead of abandoning it. That was risky but by no means impossible. The house stands all alone above its parkland of oak and elm, and the Pidge is easily reached by lanes and not more than a mile of main road. Fingerprinting revealed only mine and a gloved hand.

Our superintendent of police, while assuming that it was a hit-and-run accident caused by some quick-thinking criminal who then had the sense to return the car and clear out of the district on foot, had reservations. He said to me that my alibi was too perfect. When I replied indignantly that my witnesses were unimpeachable, he explained that he had not meant that at all, but did have an uneasy feeling that my alibi was intended to be perfect. If the identity of the car which killed Paddy were ever discovered, no suspicion could possibly be attached to me. Two conclusions followed from that: that the car thief knew for certain I would be out, and that Paddy's death was murder and not an accident at all.

He then asked who knew that I had been invited to the Pirrone party. I told him that everybody knew, but he was plainly dissatisfied with that. However, it was true. Temporary staff for house and garden had been taken on. Penminster buzzed with rumors of this dinner and dance for county magnates, financiers from the City and their offspring — hoping, I think, for TV stars and famous drunks featured in the gossip columns. Invitations had gone out a month before, and we — the local folk who were in no way distinguished but couldn't be left out — had freely discussed what we might expect and what we thought of Sir Victor Pirrone.

Some of that I told the superintendent, led on by his pleasant manner. Then the iron hand came out of the glove.

"Mr. Hollaston, to whom did you lend your car?"

I exclaimed that anyone would tell him I had no conceivable motive to murder Paddy Gadsden, who was very dear to me.

"I am not suggesting for a moment that you knew for

what your car would be used. I require to know to whom you lent it."

I gave him my word of honor that I had not lent it to anybody and added that I always left it outside the front door.

"With the keys in it?"

Well, yes, they were. It saved trouble, and the car was perfectly safe up the remote drive to the house and just below my open bedroom window. He accepted that, probably ascribing such casual behavior to the supposed bohemian carelessness of an artist, and asked me to give him in strict confidence my opinion of Sir Victor Pirrone. I replied that I hardly knew the man, that he had moved into the Manor House at the end of March and that police inquiries would be far more revealing than anything I could say. After that he left me alone.

Naturally we think we know a lot about the Pirrones. Strangers cannot settle in a little country town without becoming the subject of pub-biography, detailed and wildly inaccurate. Pirrone so far is neither liked nor disliked. He is imposingly handsome for a man in his early sixties, generous, cordial and a host out of the Arabian Nights, but one somehow feels that it might all be put on in the morning like a monogrammed shirt. He is Sicilian by birth, and it is said that he made his money in the export of fruit — then fruit to shipping, to finance, to British naturalization and eventually to a knighthood, changing his Christian name from Vittorio to Victor. Rita tells me that a more interesting side of him shows in his hobby: the social history of his island. Apparently he is a source of fascinating footnotes on the six peoples who dominated Sicily and the remnants of their customs, folklore and architecture.

Lady Pirrone I like very much on short acquaintance. She lets everyone know that she is not Italian but Spanish, and not Spanish but Basque. She rolls in fat and has not much in her still-pretty head beyond good manners inserted by a convent and excellent English by a governess. I gather that English governesses were common in the wealthy steel and shipping circles of Bilbao. She is inclined to disown industry, claiming descent from a very ancient family of Basque chieftains which, until her grandfather came down to the coast and took to shipbuilding, had never amounted to anything outside their own remote valley in the heart of the western Pyrenees — evidently a deep-rooted family much like my own, which may be why I find her congenial.

So much for Pirrone's party and my alibi. I can't be haunted by guilt. Even the subconscious has some common sense. And Meg insists that I am healthy. She'd know if there were anything badly wrong. I could detect it.

Could I? Well then, more analysis — of Meg this time as well as myself. Unlike Paddy's niece, it was not necessary for Meg to wait for probate of the will. I took her over at once. She moped for a few days and once was found looping down the High Street to Paddy's workshop. They sent for me to pick her up. No one else wanted to. She was in a chattering temper and had already bitten through the paw of an inquisitive terrier. Dogs which know her will sometimes join in her dancing, stabbing games. Cats, who set more store by dignity, always ignore her.

Both of us quickly accepted the position and I was permitted to take the place of Paddy. I had every outside pocket in my working coats enlarged to form a den for her, and she turned out to be a comfortable, undemanding companion whether I was painting in the studio or out of doors so long as she was instantly given liberty whenever she wanted it.

I wrote that Meg can see nothing wrong with me. I have begun to surmise — and more than surmise — that, through her, illness can be detected, on condition of course that one is in frequent contact with her. To start with, such contact was unplanned and as involuntary as sticking a hand in a trouser pocket; but instead of jingling coins the hand sank into the furry roll and caressed it. I have very sensitive fingers. Like the blind, I can identify textures and the nature of uneven substances without seeing them. Oddly enough this may be a useful gift to a painter. Sometimes I find that I have reproduced what I feel, thus giving another dimension to what I see.

So I quickly became familiar with Meg's bodily expression of her moods: wrigglings, rigidity, heartbeat, the tiny ears alert or relaxed, the tail stiffened to grip a ground that was not there, or used as a toy or, like a cat, as a coverlet in sleep. When that small, shrewd head was out in the open and savoring the world from the safety of the dark pocket, I began to distinguish thought and emotions much as a psychologist can acquire valuable information from the unconscious gestures of hands, eyes, head and mouth. Meg's reactions to human and other animals were at first like an unknown script, until the language of soft fur and snake ribs, of the whole graceful mechanism that drove the killer teeth, became to some extent decipherable.

My first clue to the script was accidental. Old Walter, who keeps my garden productive, is a rabbit fancier. He was showing me two of his prize white does alongside each other in their cages. Both were pregnant and near their time, and both to my eyes were exactly alike. Meg showed no interest in one but quite evidently considered the other abnormal, perhaps sick and easily to be caught. I asked Walter if she were off her food or if there were anything wrong with her. No, she was in the pink of health. Two days later she had a messy miscarriage and died.

Shortly afterwards Walter himself went down with flu, which turned to pneumonia. He had hardly ever had a day's illness and when the district nurse was in his cottage, packing him up for the hospital with the hell of a temperature and slightly delirious, he was convinced that she was laying him out for his funeral. I was standing by and tried to comfort him by telling him nobody died of pneumonia in these days except the very old.

To my surprise he muttered gloomily: "Ah, but let's see what Miss Meg thinks."

I woke up Meg, who stuck out her head and chattered. She didn't like the scent of the fever. That was all I could feel; but it seemed a splendid opportunity to raise morale.

"She says you'll be easy tomorrow," I replied.

Well, of course the antibiotics worked and he was. He is up and about now and, I know, embroidering the story. Meg has always aroused curiosity in everyone who meets her, and some of the older farmhands ask after her health with marked respect, whispering about me as they did about Paddy. The vicar, who has the usual vicarish habit of leaping in with exaggerated Christian cheerfulness where angels fear to tread, has started to greet me with: "And how's our familiar this morning?" A jest, but not so far from truth. And do I in fact receive from Meg not only with my fingers but with another sense?

I finished writing at that point. Meg was nowhere. I had been too occupied to keep an eye on her. And I had to move. The shadow had found me. Found me? No. Whatever it is, it cannot find me or lose me since it is within me.

I bolted for the open, just as earlier I had bolted for the trees. I might have gone on running till I reached the heather and the still water of the mere if it had not been for Meg. Meg must not be left behind and lost. That was the only thought concrete enough to block the nebulous, overwhelming instinct to run. Love versus instinct. It might be fair — though so doubtful, so very distant a parallel — to consider the doe who stands by her fawn quivering with terror, useless little horns lowered, while the leopard, felt but still unseen, gathers for the charge. It's a platitude that love can overcome fear, but that is not a lot of use in my case, for it does not prevent fear. Love's only business is to preserve the race, not the individual.

However, I was just able to come to a stop and call. On a fallen branch at the edge of the copse I saw Meg sitting up, herself like a lively, straight shoot growing from the dead, and she came bobbing down the hill, up my leg and into her pocket. Perfectly calm and friendly. Whatever wants to eat me does not eat polecats.

Through communion with Meg confidence partly returned. When at a crossroads of lanes I passed a small white pub with a notice of Bed and Breakfast in the bar window, I turned back and went in. Naturally they were fascinated by Meg, assuming that she was a ferret and that I was training her; I could hardly be poaching rabbits since I wasn't the type and carried neither net nor gun. When I explained that she was just a pet, all they wanted to know was whether she was clean about the house. Spotless. Polecats, like cats, will be clean with very little maternal tuition. In Meg's case, Paddy must have acted as a mother in the first few weeks of her life with him.

The landlord was a townsman; he had been a barman in a Bournemouth hotel and had not needed much persuasion when a chance came to set himself up in the peace of the country. The persuasion, I am sure, was due to his wife, who was sturdy, deep Dorset, hailing from Poyntington, not far across the county border from Penminster. She seemed to take to us and told me that my friend — as she rightly called Meg — reminded her of her grandfather, who possessed a black bantam cock which followed him everywhere and used to sit on his shoulder. My Indian owl would do that in our common bungalow but seldom followed me.

When I asked her what his neighbors used to say about that, she just replied: " 'E were a funny man," looking as if she could say more but wanted a lead from me. I must have chosen the wrong one, telling her about Meg and her habits in the hope that she would open up about the companionship, if any, of a bantam cock. She did not seem overinterested and returned to the bar.

Alcohol helps — so much that I see danger there and must be careful. I ate well and slept well, but woke up sweating with panic. I am trying to blame it on a slight hangover, but that explanation, I know, is ridiculous. The open is no good; cover is no good; even the sanity and fragrance of a little pub in utter quiet between pasture and the heathlands of Poole Harbour is no good. I might just as well go home.

# II

## June 4

I have at last made myself call on Dr. Gargary. I had refused to consider it before I ran away, being almost as afraid of his tough, hearty manner as of my suffering. I knew him only as a Penminster worthy and occasional companion, for I had never needed his services. Consequently I underrated his intelligence. I am prejudiced against the artificiality of the professional manner, whether of doctors, lawyers or priests. Unfair. I never minded the proud bearing and military panache of my Indian officers.

I ran into him at the school sports day and on a desperate impulse told him that I needed his advice and that it was not a matter he could deal with in the office. He at once asked me around to his house for a drink. There I told him as much as I thought fit, trying to play down the irresistible terror. I did not expect much skill in psychiatry from a general practitioner in a country district. Again wrong. While the specialist can concentrate on the cases where the ever-changing theories are applicable, the country doctor — in tune with the seasons and with the reluctance of his patients (so unlike townsmen) to waste time on medicine men unless in serious trouble — has to keep a more open mind.

"My dear man," he said, "let's get another fear out of the way first! You are not going mad, whatever 'mad' means. Fear of a fear is fairly common. Call them Fear One and Fear Two! Get at the cause of Fear Two and Fear One vanishes. How's Meg?"

I replied that she was fine and added without thinking that she couldn't see anything wrong with me.

"Well, we can't take her as gospel," he said.

That left me staring at him in surprise.

"I knew Paddy and Meg intimately," he explained. "Meg's diagnosis could give a lead, but she is far better with animals. Ask the vet! Did Paddy ever talk about it to you?"

He never did, at least not in detail. He did say that he paid serious attention to what Meg had to tell him. I knew more or less what he meant: that there was always a reason for Meg's likes, dislikes and reactions. A musician, for example, can spot when a concert pianist plays the wrong note; the rest of us can't. Well, Meg is an expert in the music of personality. Paddy told me little or nothing of his ability to diagnose through Meg. I found out for myself that it was conceivably possible.

22

Gargary asked if I had always had a close relationship with animals. I told him about my brown mongoose — not all that different from Meg — and my cheetah kitten and the old zebu bull who used to walk on to my verandah to share my breakfast. There was nothing odd about that, since, being sacred, he was permitted to swipe anything he wanted from any market stall or any table, but he would rest his great, ugly head on my shoulder, which impressed people, especially if it was evening and my Scops owl was occupying my other shoulder.

"You are interested in the religions of India?" he asked, skating around the edges of my problem. "Meditation, gurus, transmigration, all that?"

"Mildly interested, yes. But much more in primitive religion which is not particularly Indian."

Painting started it. A British mess would have found my hobby — as it then was — eccentric. The writing of poetry, if kept reasonably private, is permissible; but taking one's leave in hill jungles with an easel and paints instead of a gun would put a question mark over, say, one's choice of a mule track to support a flank attack. Indian officers, however, saw no inconsistency. To worship aspects of Shiva as well as Kali was perfectly acceptable.

But that is by the way. Year after year I used to stay with an old friend very loosely administering the Birhors, lost in the hills of the northeast Deccan and barely out of the Stone Age. As soon as I had learned enough of their language I began to understand all that the human animal abandoned when it turned from hunting and food gathering to agriculture. Both he and I often accompanied the tribe on hunting expeditions, eating and sleeping as they did. When I tried to sketch them I found that my quick drawings were so vividly alive that they had a quite remarkable resemblance to Paleolithic art. As for him, he

23

was so much at home that when he was dying — a bear broke the net and got him — he gave orders that he was to be buried as a clansman. The tribe obeyed, honoring his spirit with the long incantations of the shaman and touchingly laying in the grave, besides food and drink, a packet of his cigarettes, his official hat, a spear, his gun and two hundred cartridges.

After my friend's death the shaman begged me to return to his people whenever I could, saying that he would know when to expect me and himself would meet me on the track. That proved to be true. The receptors of his mind — at any rate between brothers — were as efficient as the now useless and mildewed radio. And brothers we were, for I had gladly submitted to the ceremony of exchanging blood with him. The gains were many, for I could appreciate the meaning of his rites and dogmas, and express it, for myself alone, in words. Some beliefs were absurd; for example, since his totem was the tiger, so was mine, and therefore I could not marry the daughter of a tiger. Others were not absurd, but incapable of proof. He assured me that I could receive thoughts emanating from a tiger. They may have appeared in nightmarish daydreams but I could not recognize them. When once I told Paddy of all this, he accepted to my surprise that the shaman, my tiger brother, possibly could. I prefer the word "shaman" to "witch doctor." It has the connotation of a priest caring for parishioners rather than the tatty and terrifying antics of rattling gourds, tusk teeth and painted body.

"Are you yourself religious?" Gargary asked.

"Profoundly — in the sense that I believe in a Purpose and that all life is one. *Benedicite omnia opera!*"

"Then have you any theory yourself about your neurosis? You said that the follower had no form but it was present. Is it present now?"

"It is waiting for me when I go out."

"Shall I ask it to come in?"

I am ashamed to record that I broke down there. I can see now what he was after: to find out how objective it was in my imagination. It was hardly Harley Street treatment, I am sure, to knock down all my defenses with seven words instead of an hour a week for six months.

"Would you like to tell me your own theory?" he asked when I had recovered. "A man with your inquiring mind must have one, however bizarre."

Yes, I do have one and I tried to explain it to him. It's not at all bizarre. Animals know when they are in danger; they also know when they are not. A full-fed tiger can walk past a herd, which will quietly continue to graze. I told him that he could watch the same instinct at work on the Long Down at the head of my valley if he hid on the edge of the gorse and had the luck to see one of our foxes pass through the feeding rabbits, which were aware that it had other business and was not hungry.

Now, when we were only hunted and hunters — in Europe a mere three hundred generations ago — we shared this sixth sense which told us when we were in danger and when we were not; so it is not surprising that in some of us it has never been suppressed. Big-game shikaris all agree that it exists and that they have turned aside, without any conscious reason, when they were walking on into certain death.

"That is what I think may be happening to me," I added. "That sixth sense is out of control. It is continually telling me there is danger."

"Warning you when in fact there is no danger?"

"I suppose so. But if I really believed there was none I should not be afraid. My trouble is that I believe there is."

"Farfetched. We're not animals, though sometimes I wish we were. Anyway, if you are right, I can destroy your sixth sense at once."

"How?"

"Tranquilizers. And there is a new drug to control hallucination."

I said that I should want a definition of hallucination, and as for tranquilizers, I was not going to lie about dreaming like an elephant with a sedative dart in his backside.

"Have you ever taken a tranquilizer?"

"Unless you count alcohol, of course not!"

"Yes, you are the lucky sort who has been able to produce his own up to now. By the way, you are sure it has nothing to do with Meg?"

"Quite sure. Is that why you asked me straightaway how she was?"

"Not altogether. I was just asking after a common friend to put you at ease. Let me think it over! I must revive some rather vague memories of what Jung had to say. And whenever you need to talk, I'll come around."

I have not asked him to come around. Gargary has only given me a new fear: of his drugs and their effect. Fear Three he might call it if he knew. It would be too easy to stupefy myself until I became indifferent not only to the terror which lurks at my back but to all joy and to all my striving to reveal through paint what is beyond the objects painted.

Does that devotion matter? I think it does. When the achievement is appreciated, when the world beyond the world of sight has been successfully interpreted to another, I know it does.

I can never forget that fellow Julian Molay whom Paddy sent around to see me at the end of March: one of his foreign customers whom he had been supplying for years with English hunting saddles decorated to order. He had an estate in the Amanus Mountains near Alexandretta, Paddy said, and wanted something to remind him in the dry gold of the Mediterranean that there was still grass in the west.

I exhibited what I had: some triumphant, considering how hard the gentle green curves of England are to paint, some which I disdain as picture postcards in which my craft has not failed me but inspiration has. Molay showed exceptional discrimination, and I felt he might be instinctively fastidious because he himself was such a splendid product of human maturity — tall, hawk-nosed, with a skin of fine bronze and preserving the tense vitality of youth in spite of his gray hairs. With his large and deep-set eyes, he reminded me of one of El Greco's Spanish grandees.

And so on impulse I set up for him my *Holy Well*: greens beyond browns, browns beyond greens, the shadowed water leading on into an unknown beyond the perception of mere sight.

His intent face was transfigured and he looked long as I have seen a man look into a crystal ball and follow movement. When he turned his dark eyes to mine, my pool seemed to be still reflected in them.

"In India or England?" he asked.

I replied that there was no difference. Both had entered into my vision.

Then he asked what were my prices and I told him that

27

for my best work I could normally count on three hundred guineas. He chose a study of waking cattle — no picture postcard, for the dawn mist flowed through and under the great trees of the parkland — and said: "I will buy this and pay you six hundred. Let each take half, the craftsman and the mystic!"

I did not know what to make of him except that I was sure from his gasp of admiration — a reward far beyond money — that he understood the *Holy Well* and really wanted that. I told him to leave the cattle and take it.

He would not, saying that neither he nor I had the right to put a price on it. Then, spreading his wings from the too portentous chrysalis, he laughed as if we were easy friends.

"Free to good home someday," he said, "like a foal one has bred and trained and loved but must not keep."

Gargary's tranquilizers or drinking myself into numbness, no! And what would Meg think? What a preposterous question! I put myself on a level with some maiden lady who won't let her lover stay the night because of what pussy might think. But there is more to it than that. Through Meg and my painting I am sometimes near a vision of the world beyond the world, elusive but apparently a fact.

## June 8

I took Gargary's advice on one point. With Meg in my pocket I called on George Midwinter, waiting in the genial line at his veterinary office because I felt that in that way he might allude quite naturally to whatever he knew of Paddy without any interrogation on my part.

Most of the visitors were personally acquainted with

28

Meg and those that were not knew of her. There were kind inquiries after her health and I had to invent a torn claw. The waiting room at a vet's must be the most egalitarian spot in England, where the odd dozen of customers, each with ailing animal on knees, at foot, or in basket, instantly form a club offering advice and sympathy to the neighbor. Homo sapiens is unique in showing altruism towards his fellow vertebrates. That cannot be of any value to the preservation of our predatory race. The only explanation is that we cling subconsciously to the unity we have lost.

When my turn came George Midwinter was surprised to see Meg. Instead of asking me what was the matter with her he said half humorously: "What have you been doing to her, Alf?"

To George and other close friends I am Alf, Alfgif being hard to get one's tongue around, though easy as Alfred to my Saxon forebears. I wonder if King Alfred had to put up with Alf when his thanes were on their third round of mead.

"As near as possible all that Paddy did," I answered. "I think she has managed to pull a claw."

When I put Meg on the examination table, she liked neither scene, scents nor our attitude. She arched her back and began to chatter.

"Careful!" I warned George. "She's damned annoyed."

"Well, she has never been to a vet before."

"Paddy never took her in?"

"Paddy and Meg had no need of me."

I have admired George from the first; in fact if I were physically ill myself, I'd as soon be treated by him as Gargary. I must have often talked to him about Paddy, discussing him as a dear curiosity and a fine craftsman and quite ignorant of the vet's special interest in him.

"Perhaps you needed them."

"If I ever did, I kept it quiet. I don't want to be known as a quack. What about Meg's claw?"

"An excuse, George. There's nothing wrong with it."

"I see. Paddy knew you were the only person who could use her. Who is my next patient after you?"

"Old Jimmy Farrar's cat."

"Ah, yes. I told him to come back when I had the lab report. Skin tumor. Not malignant as yet, but could be. I ought to operate, but it's the hell of a big patch to heal without a skin graft. Stay here while I see him!"

"Won't he mind?"

"Not a bit. He believes in — well, what you might call old-fashioned remedies. This will seem absurd to you, but he will think I called you and Meg in."

Jimmy Farrar used to be a hedger and thatcher, a free-lance worker highly esteemed. He still does a bit of hedging for a friend, but is too old to climb on roofs anymore. He lives all alone with his cat, his garden and a few chickens in a cottage kept as clean as when his wife was alive. A model man like his model hedges, clipped clean and laid straight for those who come after.

George explained to him that the cat might last a little while but that it was too dangerous to excise so large a growth.

"So it's nowt but an ugly wart?" Jimmy asked.

"Well, you could call it that."

"Will I try Bill Freeman?"

"If you like, Jim. No harm in it."

Old Farrar turned to me and asked straight out what we — we! — thought.

"For God's sake, Mr. Farrar, I don't know!"

"Have a shot!" George said.

"Meg doesn't like the look of it. Or it may be that I

myself don't like the look of it, and she catches it from me. I haven't had her long enough to know."

"But would you 'ave a word with Bill Freeman for me?"

That was an eye-opener. I know Bill Freeman of course. Without a doubt he can cure warts. He doesn't need any word from me. What else am I supposed to have inherited besides Meg?

I should like to tell George Midwinter sometime about the Fear, though it would be useless. He would appreciate what I mean by the sixth sense rather better than Gargary and understand my theory that it is out of control; but he too would recommend drugs. My God, I wish I could put a tail between my legs and run into the safe twilight green of tall bracken!

But I have tried taking cover where I cannot be seen and have tried wide open space where I can see for miles. I have tried everything, even an attempt at insane courage. I loaded my gun. Remembering Gargary and my shameful breakdown, I asked It aloud to come in. Nothing came. Nothing came. But the Fear redoubled. It was behind my chair. It was outside the window. It was wherever I could not see it without turning my head. I nearly committed the ultimate crime of aiming the gun at myself. I remembered in time that It would like that. Where It goes wrong is that I can formulate and define death, whereas an animal, I take it, cannot. To the animal death is a terrible, amorphous danger which the genes must avoid. I reproduce for myself the panic but can still ask questions.

Questions. What keeps me alive is a spirit of research; into the Fear; into the oddities of my past; into my relationship with Meg, which has nothing to do with the Fear and is sometimes an antidote. Gargary was barking up the wrong tree there. Another antidote, quite inexplicably, is this notebook.

Vaguely I know why Paddy left Meg to me instead of to George, who knew so much more than I about her. But surely there must have been among his friends some sensitive horseman at home or abroad who could have made better use of her? A surprising number of them turned up at his funeral as a result of the prompt announcement of his death. Nobody in Penminster knew who they were. Our police superintendent, who interviewed Paddy's executors after the accident, told me that one was a partner in a very respectable firm of London solicitors specializing in multinational-corporation business; it was he who informed me that Paddy had expressly mentioned a wish that I should take over Meg. I had done so anyway and was rather afraid that I should be asked to give her up.

The only reason may be that Paddy knew that Meg and I were close friends and so she would be sure of her dinner and a snug pocket; but I believe he was also saying to me that she might suggest ideas which my experience with the Birhors had laid me wide open to receive. I am still incompetent at taking what I call Meg's temperature readings — or not so much at taking them as at understanding what they mean.

I am very much alone with her. I cannot be social. The effort is too great when I am haunted. Haunted? I have not used that word before. It is the right one, for it is not essential to see a ghost when one can feel so vividly its presence. I do not believe in ghosts as spirits of the dead. I do believe in them as inexplicable phenomena which produce a shuddering fear in all animals including myself. Assuming that my sixth sense is out of control, it is unnecessary to postulate such an entity; but the effect is identical.

32

Yes, I am guilty of deserting my friends. Last night was full moon, and my vixen is feeding cubs and must be hungry. We have a distant and cautious regard for each other. The hunt has never caught her. I suspect that after a couple of winters in which to observe her outstanding character the Master and his Huntsman do not try too hard. She can be trusted to give them a long run before hounds lose her, and her cubs inherit the gift. I would not go so far as the half-wits who declare the fox enjoys being hunted — God knows I do not! — but I can imagine that when the terror is over she might feel a certain pride. Is there comfort in that for me?

Her earth is in a stand of larch, deep in the woodland across the stream. I never go there. I pretend I do not know where it is. I wait for her to come to me and I leave Meg at home to avoid the complication of possible antagonism between the pair.

Last night the moon shadows of the oaks which have guarded my house for four hundred years gave each tree a personality, a collective consciousness like that of a hive of bees. I belonged to them rather than they to me. Each separate column of sap and leaves and future buds stood in its pool of moonlight, life with purpose but without movement. Past the oaks, whose shadows I neither sought nor avoided, I came out onto the open silver along the stream. I alone moved through the stillness, hardly breaking it or disturbing the sleeping sheep, and sat down on a slight ridge where the vixen knows she may find me and, if not out hunting, would see me as a pinnacle of black among the gray boulders of the sheep. I had brought a still-warm rabbit for her and, in case the cubs were not yet ready to tear and eat, a fat pork belly to swell out the milk.

I remained for half an hour perhaps, motionless as if all

33

time had stopped except for the busy cilia of roots searching underground. At last she came, a slim shadow trotting down from the covert and leaping the stream, only visible as fox when she crept belly to ground towards the supper I had spread out five yards from me.

All this time the Fear had been absent. Since the night was pure radiation there was nothing to which it could attach itself. I had ceased to exist as a man; I was a molecule of the unity of earth and light. But when the vixen looked at me, slinking the last steps towards the strip of fat pork, I became the fascinated and humanly affectionate observer. The terror returned in force. I did not move head or body — had enough self-control for that — but the vixen jumped around, hair along the spine erect, and bolted. That was the end of me. I screamed and ran for the house, every oak now holding menace instead of peace.

What am I to make of it? Yet, looking back, it is so simple. An animal does not need speech or any cry to communicate its fear to another. There is no reason at all to give this vile thing a life of its own, to assume that it creates or actually is an aura of supernatural, diabolical fear into which the vixen had entered. My own fear was quite strong enough to be picked up by the receptors of her brain. It is curious that Meg should be unaffected by it. If ever she is affected, that will break me.

When I returned to the house the telephone was ringing. I picked it up. Rita Vernon was at the other end.

"Did you hear something scream?" she asked.

"No. The vixen probably."

She said sharply that I knew very well that vixens did not call and mate in June and that she was sure it was murder or something horrible. I replied, trying to keep my voice steady and ironical, that we were not living in London.

"The country isn't altogether innocent either."

"Where were you when you heard it?"

"Out in the garden moonbathing. The sound came from somewhere up the valley. Close to you. You must have heard it."

"I had the TV on."

"That's something new for you. What were you watching?"

"Some damned thing of potted violence about detectives."

A fairly safe guess, but I thought it wisest to add that I had gone to sleep.

"Why haven't you been to see me for so long?"

"I was away for a few days, and busy painting ever since."

"How's Meg?"

"In great form."

"I heard she had torn out a claw."

"Not so serious."

"Can I come over?"

"What? Now?"

There is no road between us, only a footpath running up the valley along the course of the stream. I did not want to see her and have to pretend heartily that all was well. I had my back against the wall while I was telephoning but I was not safe. I said that if rape or murder was going on down in the valley she had better wait till morning before taking the path.

"You could meet me halfway. Your vixen won't be jealous."

I had no possible reply to that. She suspected that I was in some trouble; I should only make matters worse by evasive artificialities. So I put Meg in my pocket and set out. Anything was better than my haunted house.

It was an act of considerable courage to commit herself to the night, though Rita knew our valley as intimately as I. The noise torn from my wretched throat had been human and male and could not have been shrieked by any other animal. What she feared or guessed I dared not think.

She was wearing a white skirt, so I saw a long way off her lower half flitting along the dark edge of the woodland like a cone of mist, and I called to her. When she came up she described what she had heard and asked me what on earth it could have been. I suggested that one of our local naturalists, out watching owls or nightjars, had twisted his ankle. She told me not to put on a show of raising morale.

Rita, I know, is strangely fond of me but often exasperated. She is a historian, a don at Somerville, and a glorious animal as well, quick in mind and body, fair and lightly golden. I try never to let her suspect how much I love her. She is nearly twenty years younger than I. The gap in age — and the other thing — insists that our relationship must be that of brother and sister. I remember so gladly our first meeting. I was in the process of getting rid of the farmland, and she boldly called on me — tall, intent and delightfully commanding as one who knew her own mind and could open it to a stranger — asking me to exclude the last, lone cottage at the bottom of the valley and sell it to her. Without hesitation I did. It was pleasant to think of grass and water flowing down from me to this Aspasia.

When the Oxford term is over she retires there among her books. Sometimes she tells me about her research and asks my advice. She won't take my "I don't know" for an answer and says that I am part of the land and aware by instinct of what my far ancestors would have thought. She insists that history is not about events but about what people thought — baron or yeoman or serf — and that the original sources have a value beyond the happenings which the author describes; they reveal the sort of mind a person had and thus the sort of mind his contemporaries had. When I consider the masters of my craft I understand what she means. To know the man one must appreciate not only what he painted but what he wanted to paint and couldn't — couldn't because his vision was limited by the thought of his time.

Suppose my *Holy Well* exists in five hundred years (I'll guarantee the colors won't fade); the painter who studies it will see what I was trying to do and will observe that I failed because I lived in an age drowned in too sudden a flood of material knowledge. So my mysticism will seem a reasonable and perhaps lovely shot at what to him is proved and established fact.

But this is by the way. I am avoiding what was painful: the keeping of my secret from Rita.

"You aren't ill, Alfgif, are you?" she asked.

"Meg says I am not."

I let her loose. She started to climb Rita's long leg — a desirable ladder — and was gently removed.

"And what do *you* say?"

"I may be pregnant with a painting."

"You are not worried by your own perception?"

"There's nothing mysterious about me at all."

"Isn't there? Your family has lived here since Plantagenet days. Instead of coming home you stay on in India. And when you do come home you decide to be a painter and not a landowner."

I pointed out that we had owned the land for only three hundred years; before that we were tenants of the Bishopric of Salisbury. She told me not to interrupt.

"You have a fey relationship with animals," she went on. "You go about with Paddy's familiar, and Paddy as everyone knows was a sort of faith healer for horses."

"He wasn't a faith healer. He didn't glide around with a pious expression laying on hands. He just knew a lot about horses and what makes them tick."

"And took good care not to be mysterious. So do you."

Meg, ecstatic with the moonlight, was dancing, mostly in leaps and circles and arching her caterpillar body, but sometimes taking a turn or two on her hind legs.

"She looks as if she were dancing with someone," Rita said.

"I don't know whom she dances with."

"Would you expect to? Three hundred years ago, dear tenant of the Bishop of Salisbury, you'd have been burnt at the stake and Paddy too."

Witchcraft, yes. Some of our old farmers and farmhands would nod and wink without mentioning the word, but knowing very well that ancient medical and other knowledge is not wholly lost. Example: old Bill Freeman who can undoubtedly cure warts.

Penminster, stuck to its car and its TV, laughs at such silly superstitions but has faith in flying saucers, in doctors' pills, in the remains of myth, comforting or cruel, in the church services and in herbalists who are not nearly so effective as a shaman because they omit the hypnotic dancing. Animals? If you want to understand them you must never forget that you are one. That is a built-in assumption of primitive man and an absurdity to the civilized, with a few exceptions like Paddy. He had only to hold out his hand with a few crumbs in the palm for any small bird to settle on it. I could not conceivably do that and I have never known anyone else who could.

Witchcraft in Europe must have preserved some empirical knowledge of the control of mind over matter or at least mind over mind and assumed that all life is much the same. That was the belief of my blood brother. Though he himself offered praise to the Purpose by different rites, he would have understood why a priest in a different environment attired himself in deerskin, horns and a tail — that gentle, dancing, herbivorous creature to whom the early Christian missionaries gave the title of the Devil.

Something of the sort I said to Rita. She replied that the Greeks did not consider Pan, that older incarnate God, as gentle. What about the word "Panic"?

I wonder now if she could have meant more than she said. Could she have got a lead from Gargary and then, knowing me so well, suspected some hallucination due to . . . to what? If so, she is wrong. If I were to imagine I saw Pan I should not be in the least afraid. I should welcome him with the raised arms of worship as the savior and interpreter of this Fear which is meant to preserve me and is killing me.

# III

June 12

The worst has happened. Meg now is ill. She dances no more but mopes, eating only from habit and not from enjoyment; she tires quickly of her elflike flittings and her explorations of every hole, cranny and baseboard. Oddest and most affecting is that she continually comes to me for comfort, sleeping in her pocket, gratefully nibbling the hand. Thank God it does not mean that she is receiving the Fear. If she were, she would back away from me like the vixen.

Being sure of that, I called in George Midwinter. He

said that so far as he could tell — having only experience with ferrets — there was nothing wrong with her. He could only recommend a change of diet: I should try letting her kill her own food in her own way.

I didn't confess that I had tried that, for I was a little ashamed of loosing two rabbits and a hen where they could not possibly escape from her. She had shown no interest.

"What would Paddy have done?" I asked.

"I don't know. Accepted that we all must die, I suppose."

"It's as bad as that?"

"Meg is getting on."

"Meg will die in a leap, a stab, a flash," I told him, "or killed clean."

"Well — if you know."

"Feel, not know, George. Anything so vividly, intensely alive cannot rot away like us."

"Can you still get what you called your temperature readings?"

I answered that I had not tried, and that anyway I did not know how to use Meg for diagnosis. I only saw that it could be done, which George himself had admitted.

"Any success was due to Paddy more than Meg," he said, "but Meg somehow tuned him in."

A good phrase and true. George left me obsessed by Paddy. I had to know still more about him. It seemed to me that the right source would be another practitioner of inexplicable folk medicine. I decided to call on Bill Freeman, the wart healer.

I knew him but had never been to his cottage before. It lies to the west under the shadow of the downs, all alone at the start of a bridle path worn down by pack horses and the passing of herds, deep as a green riverbed. I think it may once have been an alehouse for the drovers, and it still has a welcoming air under its thick thatch.

Bill is a little man of about sixty with a small head on a slim body and a narrow, rather puritanical face relieved by a pleasant smile. His wife looks more like the conventional idea of a witch. She is dwarfish, sharp and eccentric with dirty gray hair hanging down in ringlets, and I suspect some Gypsy blood. She has a wide knowledge of herbs; they seemed violent remedies to judge by what she told me — expectorants, ointments, aperients and so forth, mostly containing sulphur. No familiar. Far from it. Her pair of tabby cats were abused for kitchen thieving, egg stealing and leaving kittens about. The relationship was armed neutrality on both sides.

They greeted me with marked respect. I guessed that this was due to Meg and remembered how old Farrar had asked me to have a word about his cat with Bill and how I had wondered what else besides Meg I was supposed to have inherited. At first I led the conversation to Paddy, feeling that he might have taught Bill his art, though the curing of warts was not at all up Paddy's street. As Rita had said, he was at pains not to be mysterious and to be known only as an unofficial horse doctor with a curious pet.

Reminiscences of Paddy led naturally to George Midwinter and Farrar's doomed cat.

"It's a 'ard job and prayerful," Bill said. "But that evil thing is smaller than 'twere."

I congratulated him as if his report were all in the day's work, hiding my surprise at the way he had put it. Then I told him how Meg had lost all spirit with nothing obviously wrong, adding that I was sure her trouble was not old age. Again Bill's essential and unexpected Christianity came out.

"You've been given a gift for the beasts, Mr. Alfgif, and know that they ain't no better than the rest of us. So I reckon that if there's no earthly help we'll both pray for 'er as we would for a Christian. 'Are not two sparrows sold for a farthing?' " he quoted, " 'and one of them shall not fall on the ground without your Father.' "

Though I find it hard to define my religion, the farthing's worth of sparrows belongs in it provided that for Father I may substitute the Purpose, thus admitting the universal power of prayer but begging the question of identity.

Bill had now gone so far in accepting me that I could risk a direct question.

"Is that how you cure warts?"

"It's my gift, Mr. Alfgif, like old Paddy's and maybe yours. And as warts is alive there ain't no difference except that you cures and I kills."

"But how do you kill?"

"You ain't the first that 'as asked me that, and I can only tell you like I told Dr. Gargary that I just thinks about 'em and they goes."

"Who taught you?"

"Grandmother — she learned me. But never you go out to others, she said — let them as knows about it come to you! Don't you talk about it and don't you never take money for it! And you know who learned 'er?"

I didn't and said so.

"Not your grandfather Alfgif, but your great-great-grandfather, who was Alfgif too. Her 'usband was 'is shepherd."

By tradition the Saxon name has always skipped a generation. My father, Henry, for example, was a much loved man, a pillar of the district, a magistrate and church-warden with his depths as honest and simple as the surface. My grandfather, Alfgif, was an immensely successful farmer and stockbreeder. It was said of him that he had only to look at a bull calf to see that its progeny would be prize dairy cows. There must have been some vision in him beyond an experienced farmer's good eye for a beast. Great-grandfather I know very little about; he died young. And now here's great-great-grandfather, Alfgif, curing warts and handing on his skill to the wife of one of his men. It's curious. Can there be a gene responsible for this insight which skips a generation?

These ancient villages around Penminster still keep a memory of so much that I never knew or that passed clean over my head as a boy. That's what happens when a man pulls up his roots and chooses to serve a foreign government rather than his home. Paddy, now I come to think of it, must have known all this history very well, but never talked to me about it beyond a few references to my grandfather. It's as if I had been on probation.

Bill Freeman's power of prayer or meditation interested me. I did not dare to tell him of what would be too terrible and complex for his simplicity, but I did ask him if he could cure sickness of the mind.

"Not in myself or others, Mr. Alfgif. That's for a minister of religion, that is, and God be thanked for him!"

"And what would happen if you tried to kill anything larger than a wart by thinking about it?"

"I reckon nothing would happen, not if the creature was innocent as them sparrows. And 'twould be a sin. Straight evil that would be."

The more I expand his thought, the more I see that he is right. Go back to the beasts, for example. If the tiger could kill its prey merely by thinking about it instead of using skill, cunning and muscle, it would be a denial of the whole Purpose. In fact, evil.

44

Evil exists all right. It is here in the room where I sit. But it is a cloud, not a joyous creation of horns and hooves which would have pity on Meg and me.

I am tormented. I cannot help either of us. I ought to grow accustomed to this unseen hound of hell as one gets used to pain, but I never do. When it is more than usually threatening I try to hide in any small space in the dark. A little ancestral mammal taking refuge in a hole? I have even cleaned a cupboard under the stairs so that there is room for me and made the excuse to Ginny that I need a dry spot for legal and family documents.

I don't think Ginny suspects anything. Thank God my father made for her a cozy little apartment in the old stable block so that she is completely independent. In the mornings when she is cleaning I can pretend to be busy in the studio, and in the evening she is in the kitchen preparing a meal. I force myself never to miss our daily chat by which she sets great store. I too used to enjoy it, for she is as good a source of news as the local paper — indeed rather better, being unperturbed by the threat of libel.

Such healthy, earthy gossip! All this modern yap of permissiveness is a thing of urban middle classes. We have been magnanimously permissive around here since England was England; we only pretend to be shocked. In such a commonsense society, accustomed to accept enigmas in persons and houses as normal, whispers are out of character except among schoolchildren. Paddy, the town saddler, was a familiar figure who fitted his slot in country life. As for me, I am none the worse for the centuries-old reputation of the Hollastons as a funny lot. Yet to the outer world we are mysteries, not to be taken simply.

Yesterday brought the oddest proof yet. I was pretend-

45

ing to myself that I was working in the garden while Meg slept in the sun sound enough to interest a hungry crow. In full form she would have had a leg off that fellow for daring to swoop over so close. A car drove up to the front door and I went to meet the unknown caller — a fair-haired chap with one of those slightly wizened, smiling horseman's faces.

"Excuse me!" he began. "Am I speaking to Colonel Hollaston?"

I have never used the title of colonel — which proved, first, that he was a stranger to the district and, second, that he had taken the trouble to look up my past.

When he found I was the right man he introduced himself as von Pluwig, giving me the impression that he thought I would recognize the name. He was evidently German though his English was near perfect. He apologized very courteously for his call and said he believed I had Mr. Gadsden's famous Meg. I agreed that I had, jumping to a conjecture that he could be a zoologist or park director who wanted to breed polecats from her — which might be good for her health.

"I wonder if Mr. Gadsden ever spoke to you about my stable of Hanoverians at Hildesheim?"

No, I said, he had not. He was a close and dear friend but I had little knowledge of horses and so we rarely talked about his business.

"He used to stay with me occasionally."

"Yes, he once mentioned that he was going over to Germany and asked me to look after Meg. He was a wonderful craftsman and it's extraordinary how his reputation spread from this little town."

"He was greatly respected by his friends in Germany."

I wondered how he knew of Meg's existence, for Paddy

46

never took her abroad, since she would be clapped into quarantine on return.

Von Pluwig, not surprisingly, seemed embarrassed by my lack of response. So to put him at his ease I asked if Paddy made the saddles for his Hanoverians.

"No. But his understanding of horses was really remarkable."

"And he talked to you about Meg?"

"Yes, indeed. And twice I met her when Mr. Gadsden was kind enough to accompany me to hunter sales and give me his advice. Well, I am glad she has such a good home. May you both be happy in your —" he hesitated for a word — "your communion."

He drove off, after mentioning that two of his horses would be jumping at Wembley next week in the International Horse Show and that if I were free and wanted tickets for any day I had only to telephone him at his hotel.

His visit makes sense. Obviously Paddy had gone to Hildesheim as an unofficial veterinary consultant. An equine psychiatrist, I think one might call him. And I, as the possessor of Meg, was supposed to have inherited Paddy's skill.

In all this there is nothing whatever supernatural; nor is there anything supernatural in Freeman's curing of warts. He kills them by thinking about them, he says. Granted action of mind at a distance, his "thinking" is as straight an attack as X-rays — which themselves were incredible magic one week and established scientific fact the next. But can such action be granted? Well, the biologists are sufficiently convinced to experiment. And chess masters, in spite of their closed mathematical minds, seem to accept that logical thought can be endangered by observers watching too intently.

As for humanity in general, it has no doubt that telepathy exists. Action of mind on mind with a wall between them, or face to face as in hypnosis, is pretty well proved. Action at a distance of many miles seems less credible — not that I doubt for a moment the miracle of the centurion's servant. But how does the sender establish the identity and position in space of the target? And since some form of energy must be involved, where does he get the power? My blood brother could at once have answered that last question if put to him in his own terms. Power is generated by dancing and the trance.

Am I then to exhaust myself into trance in order to return Meg to the Purpose of polecats? Or can I do it no less efficiently by prayer, as Bill Freeman says? Well, unconsciously I could pray for her by using the only power I have. I shall try to paint her deep in the wood where in nature she would live.

## June 16

At first it was impossible. She would not move except for the sharp muzzle questing here and there for the joy once known, like a snake in its spring resurrection. For two days all I could catch were some impressions of the background I wanted her to enter.

On the third day, silent enough in the woodland to remind me of tropical forest, a tree creeper came to my help. It was running up and round the bole of an ash with such busy spirals that it attracted Meg's attention. She may have wanted to catch it, or the bird's excited search for food may have reminded her what a pleasure was appetite. At any rate Meg stood up against the tree and then started to sniff around in the grasses, appearing and reap-

48

pearing and once sitting up to whistle at me as if she required me to leave the easel and play, which of course I did. She was not interested, but showed a first sign of liveliness by lying on her back and putting her head between hind legs so that she could have been rolled like a wheel. My pencil caught the curve, though its sweep could have meaning only for myself.

All day I worked, still when she was still, filling sheet after sheet when she was active, concentrating on her till the sketches seemed to become a composite of what I needed, and I could begin to give life to a sinuosity of black among the dapplings of the ground. Today my portrait — if it is a portrait and not a fantasy — is finished. I fear no one would recognize Meg for what she is. That is a minor point, for I believe I have achieved again what Julian Molay so admired. Among the living things which cannot move there is a living thing which can, defying gravity and of too soft a texture to be either stump or root. But both forms of life are one.

Put it this way: If the communal life of the tree could be so distilled that its spirit was visible and mobile, that would be what I have painted. Or put it another way around. Suppose I were to paint a bee (which I can't), it would be a pretty, photographic bee; but suppose I could so paint a bee so that you saw or felt in it the spirit of the whole hive, which is the true reality — then that would be akin to my imitation of Meg.

The astonishing thing is that she has become the old Meg. Apparently I have cured her. The trance of painting must be close to the trance of the shaman. My own mind has flowed into her like the milk of a girl burnt at the stake for feeding her familiar at the breast. What am I to make of that? Is the intense, passionate concentration of the artist akin to what Bill Freeman called prayer? And if

49

it is, what wart on Meg's spirit have I killed? Speculation is all adrift. I have always been certain that Meg was not receiving the waves of my depression; but it could be that her receptors, which must be keener and more vulnerable than my own, reacted to the haunting in a different way. If so, what agency is attacking us both?

Yesterday I had a conversation with George Midwinter while he was riding down the valley on his afternoon off. He came upon me out in the open playing with Meg, who had stuck her back down a rabbit hole and was challenging me to fight her. Between Meg and the relentless presence of my unseen companion, I was completely absorbed and did not even hear George till he dismounted. Seeing Meg at her best, he was pleased with himself for having boldly declared that there was nothing wrong with her. He confessed that all the same he had been worried, since animals do not go off their food and mope for no reason.

"You're not looking too good yourself," he added. "Why not come to Salisbury races with me next week and bring Meg?"

Kindly meant, but there is no peace for me in crowds, where I cannot satisfy myself that there is no threat behind me since some person always is. So I objected that I could not risk Meg being crushed in my pocket.

"Underneath her is a good place to park our winnings. God help the pickpocket! Better than fishhooks," he said.

"But I never do win."

"Paddy Gadsden took her once, you know. I wanted to see if Meg could pick winners. He laughed at me and said that of course she couldn't, but we went."

George told me that they had stuck steadily to a good place on the paddock rails where Meg could get a close view of the horses. She could tell which was slightly off form but was no wiser than Paddy alone or any experienced professional gambler. With so many runners in the pink of condition and so many races won by only a length or two she was useless at picking winners.

"I did work out one way of using her," George said, "but it very rarely comes up. Suppose there were an odds-on favorite and Paddy or you or someone who could interpret Meg's reactions didn't recommend it, then one might be able to make a bit backing the field."

"What did Paddy think of that?"

"Not much. He said he knew the winner more often than not. And when I asked him why he didn't bet, he replied that he would never use his gift to make money. I pointed out that, damn it, he didn't give his services as a horse psychiatrist for nothing, and he replied that they *were* services like my own and on a different plane than gaining money for money's sake."

George had then objected that he couldn't see anything immoral in backing one's luck, and on his own admission pestered Paddy with questions about good and bad luck as if he had been a Gypsy. Paddy told him that luck was in the mind. If you mixed beer and water, there was no reason why the two liquids should not remain separate, each in its own half of the glass, but the odds against that happening were tremendous. If anything could make them do so, it would be the interference of mind. He added a curious remark which George remembered exactly: "One can be a director of a brewery but have no practice in pulling a pint."

I wish Paddy were alive to help me. However, I might never have told him of the haunting, for I thought of him only as very congenial company, always understanding what I was getting at and approving or illuminating my speculations with solid example. But George, who often consulted him and naturally kept very quiet about it, well knew a Saint Francis side of him which partly escaped me.

Ginny tells me that Rita has twice come around to see me and complains that I am never in. I don't know why she cannot telephone first. If she did, this nervous beast, banished by itself from the herd, could clean itself up and emerge from its chosen den of the day, always useless wherever it is.

I summoned up such remains of courtesy as are left to me and drove around to call on her. I am weary of walking and hiding in my once dear valley.

She greeted me with a cheerfulness which I could see was put on. When she had given me a glass of her college sherry — these harems of learning keep up the better traditions of Oxford monasticism — she said mercilessly (made angry, I like to believe, by affection): "You look about seventy. What's the matter, Alfgif?"

I replied that it was old age creeping up.

"You should see a doctor. And I don't mean Gargary."

"He's good enough. He assured me that there was nothing wrong with me."

"When?"

"A few days before you went moonbathing and heard a chap twist his ankle."

"Ginny is very worried about you."

So that was it — the pair of them being motherly! I thought I had completely deceived Ginny. I asked what she had said.

" 'Allus cooin' to that dratted, bothersome animal, me dear,' " Rita said, imitating Ginny's accent, " 'and no time for the rest of us.' "

"I don't coo to her out loud."

52

"She didn't say you did. I hear Meg has been ill."

"Yes. But I cured her."

"How, Alfgif?"

"By painting her."

An impulsive answer, but I wanted to see what she would say to it.

"You mean you cured yourself of imagining that she was ill?"

As so often she had offered a comment right off the expected line, and I had to stop and think about it before replying.

"Will you accept that Midwinter agreed that she was ill? That's proof of reality."

"Of course. Why are you worrying about what is reality and what isn't?"

"It's how philosophers earn their living."

"But you aren't a philosopher. You're a mystic."

"Two aspects of the same search. Both seek truth, the philosopher by logic, the mystic by experience."

"But what is the importance of Meg?"

"I don't yet know."

And I don't, beyond her possible usefulness in diagnosis. On the other hand, Paddy could do his horse healing without her presence. Meg, as I see it, was for keeping his receptors in training — tuning him in as George put it.

What do I mean by that? It's hard enough to satisfy my own curiosity, let alone Rita's. The man must become one with the animal, think as it does, dance as it does — for all have the habit of dancing with joy. He then reverts to his own primitive nature and recaptures communion. Odd that von Pluwig should have used that word!

So when I painted Meg, I became half Meg and could

affect her illness, which seems to have been psycho-somatic.

It occurs to me now that I could have given Rita quite a simple example of this wild and complex theory. Take the lonely old lady or bachelor devoted to a dog. Over the years the owner begins vaguely to resemble the dog, and the dog the owner. People say the dog is becoming quite human; but it is equally true to say that the human being is recapturing the knowledge of his far ancestors: what it is like to be a dog.

In order to half answer Rita's question and steer her away from whatever she and Ginny might be imagining, I told her how von Pluwig had appeared out of the blue because he had learned that I possessed Paddy's Meg.

"Haven't you wondered who told him?" she asked.

"The news probably went around among horsemen."

"But you have had no visits from English horsemen."

"No. After all, they have had a month to make inquiries and discover that I know nothing about horses. Von Pluwig probably hit on the idea of tracing the person who had taken over Paddy's Meg and hoped for the best."

"Wincanton!" she exclaimed.

"Wincanton is cattle, not horses. And if he had had a friend there he'd have said so."

"I wasn't thinking of von Pluwig," she said. "I was thinking back to 1664 and your great-great-grandfather."

"What on earth do you know about him?"

"Only what Bill Freeman told me."

She explained that she had had an annoying wart on her forefinger. It might have come, she said, from turning over pages of vellum manuscript, and Ginny had advised her to consult Bill Freeman. She had gone to him purely for the sake of a footnote on the persistence of tradition, but to her amazement the wart had nearly gone.

54

I waited for more, momentarily disconcerted to learn that she and Ginny were on such good terms and conspiring to nursemaid an aging artist who chose to live alone and even now was as capable of looking after himself as ever he was.

"I didn't connect your family with 1664," she said, "or Bill Freeman either."

I replied stuffily that my great-great-grandfather was not alive then.

"No, but *his* great-great-grandfather was, stretching it a bit, when the Wincanton witches were condemned in 1664. Only ten miles from here, Alfgif."

I remembered that the landlord's wife at the inn where I stayed below the Purbeck Hills told me that she came from Poyntington — just over the Dorset border and again less than ten miles from here — and that her grandfather "were a funny man" who kept a black bantam cock on his shoulder. I asked Rita if she was suggesting that von Pluwig, over in Germany, knew that some remnants of witchcraft were still alive in our district.

"No. I don't suppose he has ever heard of the Wincanton witches. It's just a chain of thought, Alfgif. Who kept track of Paddy's Meg, and why? And why should it be presumed that because you had her you too were a — what is it you used to call him?"

"A horse psychiatrist."

"Wouldn't he once have been called a witch?"

"Last time we met you said that I was one."

"I didn't. I said that once upon a time you would have been burnt on suspicion. And now tell me what the matter is?"

"I told you. Meg was ill."

"And before she was ill?"

"Tigers in the jungle."

A half-truth, not a snub. But she could not persist with her questioning. Tigers? I maintain that this terror is of the same nature: a warning that I must run or hide. But a tiger would kill me or turn aside, and either way I should have peace.

# IV

June 19

I have great difficulty in reading. When I open a book I cannot concentrate; too often I must look around to see what is waiting for me behind my chair. But I did my best in spite of interruptions to follow the record of the trial of the Wincanton witches, especially after discovering that they confessed to being instructed and comforted by a Man in Black to whom they gave the name of Robin.

The prosecution was founded on sound legal evidence of the facts, but the court never attempted to identify Robin. Of course it did not. It assumed that he was the

Devil, who could hardly be put in the dock. The witches did not deny it (loyalty or genuine belief?) and sometimes called him Satan.

They sound like some isolated and fading little tribe whose shamans have been killed or civilized, who cannot recover the rites, let alone their meaning, and flutter around like lost hens.

All that is left of the Robin, the chief of the coven, the beast-man, the incarnation of the Purpose and its joy, is my grandfather's uncanny eye at an auction of livestock, together with my great-great-grandfather's power of healing. This gene which activates the human receptors and skips a generation — what is it up to now? Well, somehow, it was detected in me through my beliefs or my words by the saintly Paddy and by my blood brother. An anthropologist or administrator or explorer would not be capable of sensing the aspects of truth behind the antics of a shaman; a hereditary Robin would be.

Apparently I *am* a witch — a free-lance witch, one might say, with few powers and only the vaguest training in the theology of animism, but possibly with the makings of a Robin. I see that in scribbling my speculations some days ago I came to the tentative conclusion that action at a distance is powered by the dance and self-hypnosis. The latter, I suppose, in more evolved religions is the ecstasy of prayer. That is beyond my reach. I have difficulty in importuning the Purpose. Since I believe in the holiness of the senses, any ecstasy of mine would be praise not prayer: the Te Deum not the Miserere. A Robin may come steaming from the Pit, horned and clawed as the prosecution believed, but can still praise the Purpose.

This written confession of faith has momentarily lifted the Fear. Praise even in adversity like poor old Job? What else has lifted it? The approach of the vixen and my own identity with her, with the oaks and the radiance of moonlight. That was in fact a passing moment of the mystic vision which, I suspect, is the resting state of animals from the butterfly to the tiger, easily to be entered by primitive man and only with long and deep meditation by the civilized.

The Wincanton trials are short of hints and tips on the use of the tame familiar. Our local witches do not seem to have had any. They used animals much as the Roman augurs, setting the scene, calling on the god and foretelling the future by the first beast or bird which turned up. I have watched my tiger brother go through a similar ceremony to predict the success or failure of a hunt when he could have done it on his own without any fortune-telling at all — just as Paddy, according to George, could pick winners.

Meg and her like become very important in other trials outside Somerset. The familiar may be supplied by the Robin or bought or just found and tamed. It might occasionally be used for healing but far more often for cursing, and petty stuff at that: bewitching the next-door neighbor's pig, stealing some much needed butter, hastening the end of some farmer down the road who was obviously dying of natural causes. All self-advertisement. If an old woman with an eccentric taste in pets could make her district thoroughly afraid of her, she was sure, in her utter poverty, of gifts and respect. My tiger brother was sometimes no better. His power to send and receive telepathically was beyond doubt, but he was not above hocus-pocus if he didn't get his proper share of what food was going.

I wish he had used a familiar; but since he believed that he could send his soul to commune with beasts in the wild, he had no need of one at home. In spite of all this reading I am still unable to answer Rita's question: What is the importance of Meg?

## June 21

Yesterday I was forced to take some interest in my fellows. I was walking up the track — once my way to the outer world and now become my protection against it — when I saw Victor Pirrone's Lancia parked near the junction to the main road. Since he was hardly more than an acquaintance and had never been in the house, I assumed that he had winced at the prospect of mud on his flashy bodywork and was walking down on some business, though I couldn't imagine how I had missed him.

So I turned back, forcing myself not to be discourteous, and then spotted him wandering along the line of great beeches which form my upper boundary and swinging a large, empty parrot cage in his hand. He explained that he had been out searching for his wife's macaw, which had escaped and taken to the air, and had caught a glimpse of it at the top of a beech while he was driving along the road.

"I hate that bird," he said, "and I wouldn't be surprised if it knows it."

His frankness and exasperation made me think the better of him. For once he seemed to be as human as he was handsome. I asked him to come down to the house for a much needed drink and then we would search for the parrot together.

On the way I remarked that it was a pity Paddy Gadsden was no longer with us, that he could certainly have called down a tame parrot, for wild birds would let him approach and hop on his palm.

"What was he doing when he was killed?" Pirrone asked.

"God knows!"

"An intelligent man, our superintendent of police!" he went on. "Of course he questioned me about all our houseguests that night, but none of them had ever heard of Gadsden. I told him that to my mind there was only one question which mattered: What was Gadsden doing on the lane at midnight? If he had an answer to that, it was ten to one that he'd know who stole your car and killed him."

I said that none of us in Penminster could even make a guess.

"Gathering herbs by moonlight?" he suggested.

"You've learned that much about him?"

"Yes. Afterwards. But in life I only knew him as a master craftsman. He repaired a vanity bag belonging to Concha. Ostrich skin and silver it was, and the handle had torn out. A Bond Street job I thought, and then someone told me that Bond Street would probably send it to Gadsden anyway. I wish I'd known he was a sort of Saint Francis as well."

"Especially with horses."

"Not the kind of thing one expects in this tidy country. I've had some experience of it, healing and all. I knew a priest in Sicily who could make goats dance. He shared his bedroom with one and smelt like it."

"A priest? Didn't that start some rumors in the parish?"

"Good God, no! It was a young billy goat, not a nanny."

I said that I had not meant that at all.

"Oh, I see what you're after. No, he was a man of great piety, outstanding piety. So there could be no question of black arts."

I remembered how Rita had said that Sir Victor was a

marvelous source of footnotes, and I asked him if there was much of that superstition about in Sicily.

"And any other you can think of! But the Church Triumphant takes witches' curses as all in the day's work."

That was interesting. He had at once connected the familiar with cursing.

"And protects?"

"Or pretends to. I never heard that cursing had any effect. I'm told that in the thirties a conference of rabbis put a terrifying packet of Old Testament curses on Hitler, and look where it got them!"

Yes, useless. By all I have read of African witch doctors, they can so upset the mental balance of any offender or enemy that he wanders off and dies in the bush, yet they are unable to affect the civilized white colonist or confident black politician. That squares with my beliefs. Urban man is immune because he has lost the receptors or they have become vestigial through disuse, and so his mind can no longer receive the message. I know nothing about Sicilian peasants, but suspect that spiritually they are still in the Middle Ages. Pagan rites and Christian rites — but the latter are firmly believed to be more powerful.

I meant to ask Pirrone about this, but we had just come out onto the lawn in front of the house when he shouted: "There's that bloody bird!" and began to call, "Leyalá! Leyalá!"

Leyalá ignored him. The macaw was standing on the coping directly beneath the apex of the pediment. The facade of old redbrick with six windows on each of the three stories — built in the late seventeenth century by some country architect doing his best with a new fashion — was too near a perfect square, so he had added a heavy pediment of gray stone matching the sills and surrounds of the windows. Any sort of frieze or decoration within the pediment would have made it still heavier, squashing the honest simplicity of the house, but my eye had always demanded some slender figure or urn or shield. That was now provided by the macaw. The metallic blues, yellows and reds of him, catching the sun, pointed the whole cubical, very earthbound house to heaven.

I longed to be able to paint him there, yet the composition would be meaningless if one could not show how the inserted miniature of color was vividly alive and glorying in its position. The macaw knew very well that he was beautiful — I don't mean consciously, though I wouldn't deny it — and was vain as a cat taking stock of itself.

I told Sir Victor to stay where he was and walked across the lawn, devoutly thanking Leyalá for his gift: a silent act of worship towards the Purpose displaying itself in an individual. I think I also lifted my arms towards him in the hieratic gesture, but cannot be sure of the exact movement with which my body intensified the concentration of my mind. Leyalá took off from the coping, planed down without a flutter of wings or tail and settled on my shoulder. When I consider it now, I am amazed; at the time it seemed inevitable.

The bloody bird, as Sir Victor had called him, lived up to his name and ripped Pirrone's hand open when he tried to grab him. I suggested that Leyalá had probably had enough liberty to know whether he enjoyed it or not, and would sit quietly on my shoulder.

"He can't travel loose in your car," I said, "and he isn't going back to his cage without protest. Let's have that drink and telephone your wife to drive out and get him."

We found Ginny cleaning the living room — or rather playing with Meg. She was delighted and surprised to see the three of us and exclaimed at this gorgeous paintbox of a bird who was chortling away to himself as if amused by his position. I patched up Pirrone's hand, poured out some whisky for us and asked Ginny if she had anything fit for the other distinguished guest. She could only suggest the first raspberries, which she had picked that morning with the dew on them. Leyalá put his foot on the edge of the bowl, deliberately upsetting it. He liked to see the items of what he was offered, not to sink his bill into a mess of crimson porridge. Highly approving, he scoffed the lot.

Meg, fearless and curious as ever, jumped onto the table. She cannot, George tells me, see color, but she must have been amazed at such a riot of unbelievable grays. The macaw whipped around and Meg did a vertical take-off over that formidable bill with the spring of a mongoose avoiding the strike of a cobra. I never before saw her do that, since she has no enemies. As she was about to close in for the kill I put her in her pocket, where she clenched her teeth on my hand instead of the macaw's spine, even so only denting the skin. Leyalá returned to my shoulder, where he remained in deep thought and then anointed my back with a remarkable turd of red and white which reminded me of squeezed toothpaste. Evidently I was being reproached all around for well-meaning officiousness.

I asked Pirrone where the musical name of Leyalá came from. He told me that it was Basque and that the bird had been given to Concha by her godfather, a farmer who owned a slice of mountain not far from the French frontier and was something of a traveler when he was not hidden among his precipices and pastures.

That led me to the question of how two persons from such remote corners of Europe had met and married. Pirrone reveled in telling me, himself amused by the strangeness of fate. As a young shipping clerk in Port Said he had been formally interned by the British at the outbreak of

war and then released to join Intelligence as an interpreter when we invaded Sicily. He had made powerful
friends, especially among members of the Mafia whom the
Americans had let loose in their homeland, and after the
war had roared ahead in the export of fruit and fruit
juices. Then he and his partners decided it would be
worthwhile to own a couple of small ships of their own.
Yards were full of orders, but Spain could supply. So he,
as the shipping expert and linguist, visited Bilbao and
came away with long-lived ships and an incomparable
wife.

"She brought me luck and love with it," he added.

It was not long before Lady Pirrone turned up. I had
talked to her at the party on the night of Paddy's death,
but otherwise had only exchanged the odd word when she
stepped out of her chauffeured car to shop, sometimes
asking my advice.

She bounced on little-girl's feet at her Leyalá, swamped
him with endearments and reproaches in Basque, and put
him back in his cage with a thrust of the bosom to which
she was hugging him. The macaw did not object. The
game was up. Her good Victor then burst into his story,
gestures of despair accompanying the account of his
drive, gestures of relief at sighting Leyalá in the tree,
arms thrown open in affection to describe his meeting
with me, hand shading his eyes as we spotted the bird on
the coping, and at last, wonder, expressed as artificially as
any opera star, when Leyalá planed down to the wizard.

Concha Pirrone thanked me prettily and asked if I too
was a bird lover, by which she meant caged birds. I replied that all of us, human and animal, could understand
some of the meanings of the song and chatter of wild
birds and added — to avoid any suggestion of criticism —

that of course a tropical splendor like Leyalá had to be caged, specially fed and kept warm. "But no doubt he was getting on fine in this weather. How did he escape?"

"I often let him loose in my boudoir," she said, "but I always see that the window is shut. And it *was* shut but I was dreamy and opened it. So silly! I don't know what came over me."

She explained that she had not had Leyalá very long, but often knew what he was thinking. Her dear godfather had assured her that the bird would take care of her if she would take care of him. Leyalá was just like a grandchild. At that point Sir Victor, embarrassed by the way his Concha was making a gushing fool of herself, got up to go. Both of them very warmly invited me to come and see them whenever I liked.

Everyone has heard such sentimental silliness from any Lady Pirrone drooling over her Pekinese, her cat or her budgerigar. But I am obsessed by the parallel of the witch trials. She is given a familiar by her Robin, told to take care of it and it will take care of her, and she claims to know what it is thinking. How well it fits! But I am sure that neither Pirrone is a member of a coven, if covens still exist. Sir Victor is a hardheaded businessman believing in nothing much but his own ability and technical progress, and she, I think, would be less gushing about her relationship with Leyalá or more mysterious.

However, she is really in close communion with her pet. She is unaccountably "dreamy" and opens the window though she is well aware that Leyalá is in the room. Order from the bird? Nothing supernatural about that if her primitive receptors were open for business. I can receive simple requests from Meg without seeing her eyes or touching her. But how was the familiar used for cursing?

66

I am certain that Paddy never cursed anyone in all his life.

Communication from animal to man is, for me, proved. But what about man to animal? My vixen does not count, for she was partly attracted by food. Sheep dogs do not count, for they obey signals and are trained till they know the game by heart. Leyalá is dubious evidence. He may have just known that I was a friend, which certainly implies some transference of thought, though not hypnosis at a distance or any detailed command.

Tiger brother in some curious way involved an animal spirit in his healing; but so far as I know he never attempted — with one exception — to influence an individual live creature. The witches, according to their confessions, did. They claimed in court — a sane, seventeenth-century court proceeding with legally acceptable standards of evidence — to be able to curse through the familiar without ever explaining and possibly not understanding what the familiar had to do with it. If the Fear will give me an interval when it is controllable — it was in abeyance during most of the Leyalá incident — I am going to try out my powers in the tradition of a witch.

Among the little paradises of my home is a bullock's paradise: forty acres of emerald grass, starting at the wide mouth of a dry valley in the downs, where the land changes from short turf only a hand's breadth deep over the chalk to meadows filled by the silt of some prehistoric flood. This rich beef ground was acquired by great-great-grandfather and sold by me to William Hutchins, who has just bought a fine bunch of Angus steers for fattening, strangers to the place and still nervous. Now let us suppose that I was an old wise woman whom Hutchins had turned out of my cottage — he's a good farmer but just the blinkered type of go-getter who wouldn't have hesitated — and suppose I had a bitter grudge against him; then I would make one of his lovely beasts break its leg. Without going so far as that, let us see if it can be done.

## June 23

It can. Around four o'clock yesterday afternoon, when the sun was at its hottest, a score of beasts were grazing or gathered on the beaten earth under the shade of a big sycamore. I was some fifty yards from them downwind and completely hidden by the hedge. The thorn was thick in its third year from laying and the ditch on the far side was deep. To stop any cattle getting down in the ditch and eating hedge or trying to force a way through, Hutchins had fenced it with three strands of barbed wire to a height of some four feet.

At that distance my field glasses showed the colors of the ear tags and some of the numbers. From the group in the shade I chose a powerful little beast with a proud and gentle curly forelock, Red Tag 43, and put the glasses back in their case.

Tiger brother taught me how to surrender to trance. Even in that mild form, without the accompanying dance, I dislike it. Very different is the holiness of self-hypnosis produced without intention and akin to the mystic vision of unity. However, I used the tiger-brother technique, willing the bullock to leave the group and come towards me. "Willing" is the wrong word; it implies master and servant. It would be truer to say that I surrendered or tried to surrender to the oneness of me and the bullock.

It blew through its nostrils but that was all. I then took Meg from my pocket, who at once climbed to the top of my head to see what I was stalking with such intentness. I raised both hands so that my fingertips were in her fur and again transmitted to the bullock. It left the group, slowly and doubtfully walking towards me. Then it began to trot with head lowered, charged the wire, broke it and subsided into the ditch. As if I were the stockman bringing hay, the rest of the herd straggled after it, but with a difference in bearing. Their heads were lowered and they appeared more ready to repel than to receive. The unknown beyond the hedge was a danger, not a friend.

I was appalled at what I had done, for the bullock was rushing up and down the ditch unable to find the gap in the wire that it had made and might well break a leg in good earnest. I could not force a way through the hedge, so I showed myself and followed it, quietly talking. That calmed it down. It did not connect me at all with the summons which its receptors had answered; I had become a well-meaning, everyday human being. With the aid of a long stick and an occasional poke through the hedge I guided it back and out through the gap in the wire.

I can draw some tentative conclusions from the experiment. As an analogy it may be helpful to think of the familiar as a transformer station, one of the little redbrick huts one sees outside villages to reduce the voltage, though it is not voltage which needs transforming. The bullock can hardly receive me on the human wavelength, but can receive when it is modified by Meg.

A second conclusion is most curious and unexpected. It was Red Tag 39, not the intended 43, which came to me. This indicates that even at close range the target cannot be identified with certainty when it is nameless or not conscious of any name. The simplest form of witch's curse may therefore be in the nature of a broadcast.

The aggression of the beast I can only explain by the

assumption that it felt the signal received was "evil," which I may perhaps define as deliberate abuse of love. There is a faint parallel with my own bouts of terror, but I cannot believe that I, like the bullock, am being "cursed."

## June 24

This evening Gargary dropped in on a casual visit to see how I was. He told me he had been refreshing his memory of Jung but could not really understand him and was left wondering if such a thing as perfect mental health existed. If it did, he thought, it would exclude so much on the borderline that little individuality would remain; so nobody — meaning me — should be worried at divergence from the norm. Should accept it with pride, I suppose! Very questionable advice for the insane. But sane I am, though a haunted, hunted beast.

I guessed that he had not just called to comfort me with Jung, and I wondered who had been talking to him about me. It turned out to be Sir Victor, who had treated him to the macaw story while Gargary was attending to a small boil which spoilt the beauty of his undeniably noble Italian forehead.

"How did you do it?" he asked.

"A silent call," I replied, "like the dog whistle that human ears cannot hear."

He reminded me of myself questioning tiger brother. If I pressed him too hard he became incoherent and frantic, having no words to explain what intuitively he knew. But an amateur such as I am knows so little; he can only accept. It may be that the Robins of old also found difficulty in defining and, like the court, fell back on Satan for explanations.

70

"But not carried by sound waves?"

"No."

"And conscious?"

"If you mean do I have a repeatable technique, again no."

"I thought not. But surely the collective unconscious doesn't include animals?"

"What else are we? Didn't you study biology?"

"You make no allowance for the human brain, Alf."

"I certainly do. It has to be switched off."

"Not concentrated and directed as in hypnosis?"

I avoided the question and asked him what doctors thought about hypnosis.

"A fact and a useful aid," he answered, "but medical science cannot come near describing the mechanism. It's obviously connected with telepathy, yet it's the fashion to deny there is such a thing, though any general practitioner can give a dozen instances of it."

He asked me if my anxiety neurosis was wearing off. I told him that there seemed to be more lucid intervals but that when I was haunted it was worse than ever.

"You are sure that it can have nothing to do with Paddy's Meg?"

"You asked me that before. Nothing. Meg gives me joy when I'm capable of having any. And it's her close companionship which helps in — well, whatever I did to the macaw."

I did not mention the bullock or my ancestry or witch trials. He was honestly trying to feel his way without any medical signposts, and I did not want to provoke a reaction of disbelief which would interrupt his line of thought.

"Don't take this seriously," he said, "but it occurs to me that if you can send a signal by your dog whistle which isn't, you should also be able to receive."

"I can from Meg and possibly I could from any other intimate pet, but not otherwise."

"When you came to me in such distress, you had a theory that your fear had something in common with the sixth sense of an animal — or man, if it comes to that — which warns that deadly danger is very close. I suggest that you are receiving more than you are aware of. And the sixth-sense warning is exactly and literally what you are receiving."

"But that implies a sender."

So simple a statement, yet it brought the cloud into the room and I leaped from my chair upsetting our drinks. I could almost hear Him or It crying: "Ha! ha! So now you know!" It was the absurdity of that, the overdramatization of a nothing, which made me sit down again, trembling but managing to control the incontinence of bladder and mind.

Gargary was splendid.

"Well done! You're as sane as I am, Alf, and the hell of a lot braver. Yes, it does imply a sender. let's accept that, but what about it? It's not a bogeyman out of a nightmare. It's a temporary illness. And, you being you, you might have caught it off the collective fear of a rabbit warren. One or more of the community must always be in danger."

Ingenious and perhaps just possible. Ever since his remark I have been searching past and present life for the transmitter but have not hit on anything. Distance rules out the Birhors, and in any case no signal from my tiger brother could ever produce terror.

Gargary shifted his ground to the effects of sexual deprivation, reminding me that chastity in religious fanatics traditionally led to hallucinations. Did I wish to

72

discuss the matter? I did not. That's my own business. I am not chaste from choice.

I wish I were a Robin of old days and Rita the maid of my coven. The meetings seem to have been so simple and merry. In some secure and utterly deserted site — harder to find today — a feast of meat and drink was provided by the Robin and laid out on a white cloth. After a prayer to some manifestation of the Purpose, he comforted and helped any in trouble. Orgies? Somewhat exaggerated, I suspect, by envious villagers, but it is likely that there was mating in the summer dusk. I can imagine my studious Rita galloping on her broomstick like a child, pretending she flew and perhaps believing it under the influence of my elixir of aconite and belladonna. But if on the holiest days I put on my hide and horns and tail I should be disqualified. I could not present the wreathed and formidable instrument of fertility.

Deservedly incapable! When I married my girl of liquid topaz, my nymph of the Godivari twining herself about me as if I, poor, passionate, human wretch, were Krishna and she the milkmaid Radha, I should have remembered day and night that she was little more than a child and weak from old fever. I did not remember till that dawn, two weeks after our marriage, when I woke to find her dead.

Among the Birhors my medical adviser — long before he admitted me to brotherhood — was both puzzled by my impotence and compassionate. Neither his drugs nor his incantations had any effect. Also I could not and would not dance myself to exhaustion — one of the few remaining inhibitions of my urban self — and allow him to exorcise the larval spirit which, he assured me, had taken up residence in my body. He was right. I was in-

73

deed possessed, first by uncontrollable sorrow mixed with guilt, then by my determination to lose myself in the far origins of all religion and to symbolize them in art.

Tiger brother dismissed as unintelligible my more formal landscapes with the same scorn that an art critic would dismiss the picture postcard; but when I had been inspired to shadow obscurely the true spirit of the mountain jungle and the holiness of life in plant and animal, he would see at once what I was after and exclaim that it was the truth. So he came to respect my larval inhabitant, saying that I must be patient until its metamorphosis, when I would be possessed by the splendor of the butterfly. In fact he was aware as any monk of the spiritual force of chastity. Damn Gargary and his hallucinations! Would he call the mystic vision hallucination? My blood brother did not. He perceived that there was power in reserve.

Power in reserve! Yes, in a past self perhaps, but not this present. I have nothing in reserve.

74

# V

June 25

I could not keep Rita outside my sinister privacy any longer. I went to her with no such intention, only with a learned question. Truth to her is never simple; she is so soaked in the unbelievables of the Dark Ages that she neither accepts nor rejects. My question concerned the Norse shamans. It seemed to me that they understood the full use of the familiar while Saxon and Celt were content with sticking pins into a wax image baptized by the Robin. The baptism of course was merely to name and define the target. Transmission of thought was the real weapon.

I found Rita in her study, where I stood with my back against bookshelves, refusing on some silly excuse to sit down. Quietly she set a high-backed chair in the corner so that my back and right were protected while she herself sat at my left. She had no need to say anything. My secret, via the observant Ginny, was out.

Her beauty was enhanced by big eyes behind big, clear glasses, which from force of donnish habit she would put on and off. Her air of tall, Hellenic serenity is contradicted by humor and uninhibited speech. She was irresistible, and I told her of my illness, omitting the worst of the humiliations, such as my scream of terror.

Till then all she had known of me was that I painted, had been long a widower and that during my eighteen years of service to the government of India I had spent my leaves with a tribe which had hardly evolved beyond the stage of hunting and food gathering. Much of that I expanded for her, and added the capture of Leyalá — of which she had heard like everyone else — and my private experiment with the bullocks.

"And they came to you but were afraid of you?" she asked.

"Quite rightly."

"You should get rid of Meg."

She and George and Gargary all find something unnatural about Meg which might be affecting me. They are as absurd as the shocked prosecutors of the Wincanton witches.

The grace and gaiety of my familiar are far from unnatural. When she rolls and dances and sits up with forepaws hanging down in the way of a begging dog but infinitely more alert, she takes part in the blessed playfulness of the Purpose. Since her illness she is keener than ever on fun, following me and asking me to play when I

76

have no heart for it. I am like a father overcome by melancholy whose child cannot understand why play should have become only an imitation when it used to be fast and innocent as between two children. She likes to jump for my cupped hands and be caught, then thrown onto a pile of straw from which to jump again. This was becoming a little too rough and she has invented an alternative. She burrows backwards into the straw until she is invisible. Then my hand has to attack. The black head shoots out with open mouth and she closes her needle teeth on a finger, checking the speed of the jaws so suddenly that there is not a mark on my skin. She can never have enough of this.

I tried to explain to Rita — can she be jealous of Meg? — my theory that the familiar kept the human receptors in good order, and Gargary's suggestion, more entertaining than possible, that as a result I might be vulnerable to the collective fear of a rabbit warren.

"That would be what your Norse shamans and the sagas called a 'sending,'" she said. "I always thought it meant a sort of portable ghost."

It may have done. Because a ghost is seen, it does not necessarily have objective existence. An inversion of time? A mistranslation by the brain of signals from the eye? Tiger brother, always on cautious terms with ghosts, insisted they were spirits of the dead. Well, he naturally would. It is impossible to explain the difference between subjective and objective to hunting man who considers that matter and spirit are aspects of the same reality — though he wouldn't express it that way. What we call reality is to him only an artificial pigeonholing of scraps from the unity of life.

I told Rita that it would be easier if I were pestered by a visible ghost. I could not avoid the accompanying terror but I could control it. My sending is the cloud of terror without the ghost and I can't control it because there is nothing to control.

"Which will teach you to monkey with black arts!"

"There aren't any. I monkey with the senses which are common to all animate life. We don't use them only because we can't."

She said that she longed to be able to help me and that I must forgive her if she questioned me on the facts as she would one of her students who was onto some original idea and could not quite spit it out.

"Alfgif, have you any religion?" she asked. "I mean, beyond describing yourself as Church of England."

"I believe in a Purpose which may be called God. I could easily be a Moslem except that I am too much of a pagan for Mohammed. But Christ and Saint Francis would understand me without, I hope, condemning."

I should have been at peace in those ancestral days when it was possible to respect the Old Religion, older than Saxon or Celt, without rejecting Christianity. In that middle ground I stand and I give a profounder meaning to the legend of Saint Hubert, who, when he came up with the stag he was hunting, had a vision of the Cross between its horns.

"Then have you tried prayer to dismiss the cloud?"

I had but it was not answered. How could it be? Fear is a gift of the Purpose for our preservation. I could not ask that it be taken away from me. If it were, I should cross Penminster High Street without looking at the traffic.

"Rita, I cannot demand. I can only give praise."

"That should be enough to fix the cloud."

"It does when I feel so intensely a part of nature that I am on the edge of the mystic vision, but only for the moment."

"Is that what you meant when you told me you had cured your precious Meg by painting her?"

"Yes. The concentration of the craftsman can't be all that far from the trance of the healer. I became a part of Meg and Meg of me, and I sacrificed to the Purpose by offering my mind instead of my body."

"You sound like a twelfth-century Cathar. You haven't thought about going around on all fours, have you?"

I replied that I had not only thought about it but done it. It was supposed to be an effective rite before a monkey hunt.

"You ate monkeys?" she exclaimed in disgust.

"Certainly we did. And I wanted to see if reception from the monkeys was better on all fours than standing up."

"And was it?" she laughed.

"I don't think so. But I remind you that in addressing the Purpose we crouch on our knees and a Moslem goes down on all fours."

"You'd make an archbishop's hair stand on end, Alfgif! But if you really feel that painting can heal like the trance of a medicine man, why don't you paint this Fear and give it shape?"

When I had left her, refusing to be accompanied home like a cripple, I climbed up into the wind and space of the open downs, clear of the tender woodland but not of panic. Meditating on the bullock experiment I realized that it had been "evil" — a gross misuse of the saving power. I made them afraid. They did not know of what. Heredity warned them of the tiger crouched for the charge, the poisoned arrow, the king cobra equally afraid but unable to escape. They tended to mass with lowered heads, demonstrating that whatever killed would be trampled by the herd. Quiet Angus bullocks? Yes, but their instincts were formed when they were wild cattle, as ours when we were still wild men.

It follows that my Fear also is "evil" — the opposite of the Purpose — either brought on myself by myself or a sending by some external agency. Tiger brother would have attempted to exorcise it by the symbolism of his diagrams drawn on the ground with rice flour: that magic circle which has come down to us from the Old Religion and decayed into ridiculous hocus-pocus. It repels nothing, but tranquilizes the mind in the center and protects it from itself. Alternatively he might have been able to hypnotize me into giving the Fear an imagined form and to thus disperse it. I can conceive of it as a random nebula wandering through the community of nature. If it is condensed, it can be attacked. So my painting will not be a spell protecting me from nothing, but a circle of concentrated mind which confines a something.

I shall not choose trees and their shadows again. That was Meg's environment. Mine is the downland where the ancestral Robins held their feasts and gave thanks for all life and for their land.


## June 26

I set up my easel on the green fort where the earliest rampart had been mounded by my Neolithic forefathers whose religion, in its deepest sense, I share. Nothing was in sight but sheep, a barn and the rolling grass, so that any shape formed by my imagination would be distinct even if indefinite. But in such a landscape there was no inspiration. A rough pencil sketch of wavy lines, like a cartographer's aide-mémoire, was the truest representation of it. As on that day upon the Purbeck Hills when I had run away from home, the threat of danger was unbearable. I had wished to challenge it, but it won.

## June 27

This time Meg was with me. When the Fear climbed up the rampart to haunt me she was disturbed. She sat up, still and slender as the black, burnt stump of a sapling, searching the distance towards which I had been looking — when I was not glancing behind me — to find out what had alarmed that great creature, her companion. I was holding on to myself so tightly that I never saw the dog which came bounding silently up from below and tried to break Meg's back with one clean snap of the jaws. The first I knew of it were its desperate yelps as it tried to shake off the black demon, unwisely mistaken for a rabbit, whose teeth were clenched in its nose and whose body was swinging and flying as carelessly as a child on a mad merry-go-round, meanwhile wafting over the hilltop the fiendish stench of the defending polecat, which she had never released before. I jumped to the rescue of all concerned, and when Meg saw that I held the whimpering dog firmly by the collar she condescended to let go.

I was cheered by her example. It would be useless to direct a sending of fear at her; the most that could be done against her would be to deprive her of joy. Realizing that this was exactly what had been done, I caught the red fury of Meg's mood. Revenge. Not a pretty thought, and empty. Revenge against what?

I returned to my easel and wondered how one would paint anger. But who could concentrate on anger when the land was spread out in the sun with long arms of the hills behind its head? For the moment Fear had run off with the dog, its tail between its legs.

## June 28

Today was hopeless. Best idea: a something forming from the earth as if the birth of a volcano were interrupting the flow of the downs. But while I was dreaming on the craftsman's bridge between the vision and hard reality, I was interrupted by some damned fool striding through Somerset who sat down and wished to discuss abstract art with me. I told him there was no such thing — the only quick alternative to landing myself in a professorial attempt to define "abstract." After all, there is nothing more abstract than a map. If I had known how to use Meg for cursing, he would have been a helpless target. I was glad to see that when he was trotting down the rampart at too hearty a speed for his age he tripped, fell flat and went off limping. Perhaps his receptors were in surprisingly good order.

No peace thereafter. I wish to God this thing would finish me if it can. I am afraid of everything but death.

## June 29

Rain today. When it cleared I tried again. With the wrack of cloud sailing overhead I saw that I had been blinkered by confining imagination to the earth. It was sky bounded by earth which mattered, not the other way around, and decidedly not a study of sky alone.

Blake. I must remember Blake. But how near blasphemy he was to show Purpose in human form, though I must admit that the priest who tried to show the brotherhood of life in his vestments of horns and tail was little better. One excluded the holiness of the senses; the other

82

the splendor of unlimited mind. Both mixed too much fear with reverence. I am clearer now. Tomorrow I want worship with no fear at all.

## June 30

By God, we're off! To paint from the height of the rampart was wrong. The mass comes into the composition somewhere, but whatever represents the self must not be on top of it. The whole land was patterned in pools of dark green and pools of gold as the searchlights of the sun struck it through the clouds. Blake again. But instead of descending, cannot Life travel up the beam to reach the point of light? All very pretty, but we arrive at only an aircraft's view.

No, Robin and his earth must still be one. I shall paint the pools, but the shafts of light will be cylinders not triangles. One of them contains the self and the cloud is powerless against it, for it is in a void. Sounds crazy. This note and the dense shading of a preliminary sketch are only to make me analyze what I think I mean. As always I long to offer an act of worship, not to demand.

The painting which exorcised Meg could have been done by Pan if Pan gave up his pipe for the brush. This will be a different form of exorcism. The cloud of Fear cannot be painted, as Rita suggested. It cannot be painted because it has ceased to exist.

## July 6

Four days ago it was finished and I am still free. Can this strange and glorious normality last? I must have faith that it will, but be on my guard. Meanwhile I should profit by the new clarity of mind to refine some more traditional, less demanding method of defense.

I cannot give this work of mine a name. If asked what it means I could not answer so easily as for my *Holy Well*, which is only a picture of a pool with an unseen tenant and means no more.

But this one is a devotional fantasy. I can explain what is beyond and between these curious columns of sunlight. Beyond them is a down in Somerset which never ends and never can.

"And the columns, Mr. Hollaston?"

"Each column is a Jacob's ladder and those shadows within may be — I am not sure — forms of life neither at the bottom nor the top but safe within the emanation of the Purpose. Do not bother about them! It is an imaginary landscape, and if you like it, you like it."

"But, Mr. Hollaston, the thing haunts me."

"I too, my dear sir, was haunted when I painted it."

Up there beside the green fort I conceived a passing thought of revenge against nothing and rejected it. I reject it no longer. The reminder that in defense one must never neglect counterattack is due to Rita.

I asked her to lunch after Meg and I had celebrated by stealing out in the late twilight to catch a dish of crayfish, to which Meg, regardless of the season, had added an unsuspecting mallard grabbed with a leap as it rose from the rushes. The invitation seemed to have happily surprised Rita, and when I showed her my *Columns of the Sun* there were tears on her cheeks. She did not examine it closely, so I think her emotion was due more to my eyes and bearing. Ginny, who is fascinated by my drawings but can't abide them funny pictures, was also inclined to be tearful. It appears that I am like a botched work of art, cherished because it has been over the mantelpiece for so long.

After lunch we sat in the garden and Rita again pressed on me her theory that the depression from which I had suffered could be a backlash from the sort of powers I was using. I denied that I had any more powers than the rest of us. I merely knew they existed because I had been on terms of close friendship with a shaman.

"The difference between you and the rest of us is that you appear to have them," she said.

I told her that nobody could seriously believe anything of the sort. She then announced, merry and mocking, her hands setting the scene for me, that she would have another small brandy and put me on trial in 1664 by acting as prosecuting counsel within the beliefs of the time. I reproduce it as best I can:

"Prisoner at the bar, you are charged on suspicion of the felony of witchcraft to the great offense of God's Law, hurt and damage of the King's Subjects and to the Infamy and Disquietness of the Realm. Upon the first charge of bewitching Master William Hutchins's bullocks, how say you now to His Lordship and this jury — Guilty or Not Guilty?"

"Guilty, your worships, but not with intent."

"So now to the second charge, sirrah, of possessing an imp in the likeness of a polecat which you did nourish with your blood. How say you?"

"I never did."

"Call Mistress Rita Vernon. . . . Mistress Vernon, tell us whether upon the fourteenth June last you did not witness this abomination!"

"I did indeed witness it, good sirs."

"Damn it, Rita! Just because I once let Meg lick up the blood where she had scratched me with her claws!"

"Silence in Court! Guilty or Not Guilty?"

"Well, on a technicality . . ."

"The third charge is that you, Hollaston, did receive visits from the Devil and swore to be his servant. Dare you say you are Not Guilty?"

"If counsel is referring to Robin's chasuble of animal skin and tail, or to his appearance as the Man in Black when dressed as any other priest for visiting his parishioners, I deny having received any such visits and know nothing of the organization and practice of the religion. I confess to having been visited by an incorporeal devil, but against my will."

"Most damnable! And there is yet a fourth charge which he cannot answer, for examination showeth that he beareth upon his upper arm the mark by which the Devil claimed him as his own. How now, Hollaston? What say you to His Lordship?"

"My Lord, I have indeed been initiated by a mark, but see no more harm in it than circumcision or scarring of the face. I confess to the formality of an exchange of blood with the local representative of the Divine. His conception of sin, my Lord, was much the same as yours, plus a few extras. The scar upon my upper arm remains because herb juice was rubbed into the cut to keep it suppurating. And how the hell did you know, Rita?"

"Because Ginny told me. Silence in Court! Not only does the prisoner confess to abominable practices but would persuade us that they resemble those of Holy Church. Let him to be taken out and hanged by the neck until he is dead!"

Well, it must be fun to be alive to past and present, and

a beautiful woman with it. But now she took the wrappings off the parcel.

"Will you admit, Alfgif, that you could be taken for a sorcerer?"

"Not unless you would call Paddy Gadsden a sorcerer, which he certainly wasn't."

"Your von Pluwig thought he was."

I said that was putting it far too romantically. Paddy's receptors interacting with nature were more sensitive than mine, but that did not make him a sorcerer. And who in the world, apart from a few of the more superstitious, could possibly think that I was?

"Somebody who in fact can use the powers you only experiment with. Somebody like your tiger brother brought up to date, so that your horrible sending wasn't a freak like Gargary's rabbit warren but a quite deliberate attempt on you."

I had to agree that at least it was possible, since I was not invulnerable like skeptical urban man but receptive as a tribesman whom the witch doctor can influence to die.

"I have no enemies so far as I know."

"Then find him, her or it," she said.

Absurd! Am I blacklisted because I haven't joined the union? A joke when I put it that way. Yet tiger brother did not approve of competition. He would not admit that he had anything to do with accidents, but they happened — just as to that harmless chap boring me with his chatter about abstract art. Concentrated venom could at least distract his thoughts to the point of tripping over himself. And is there any more deadly method of distraction than to make the mind consume itself, obsessed with terror?

What alarms me in the witch trials is that the judges — one can't answer for the juries — were able men experienced in distinguishing truth from falsehood and misrepresentation. Acquittals, light sentences and pardons were frequent. Accusations plainly deriving from malice or superstitious illiterates were thrown out. So what is one to make of the death sentences?

Leave out Satan and his imps, and the evidence is as straightforward as in any police court — clear, factual and obeying the rules such as they were. Wincanton witches were guilty of using a baptized image for cursing; witches of East Anglia used the familiar. Both could also heal, but not much is recorded about that. In any case, healing by means of incantations was considered no less a crime than cursing.

I can follow the baptism of the wax image. It pinpointed — a sinister word in this connection — and named the target so that you didn't harm bullock 39 instead of 43; then dancing or trance provided the energy for transmission.

Now a step further. The human mind can in quite common experience influence an animal; therefore the opposite ought to be true provided that the human receptors are not atrophied. However, the target must be identified and in the neighborhood. Tiger brother vaguely claimed to be able to receive from animals in the immediate district. He would never have claimed to be in rapport with an elephant in Ceylon.

What would be the effect of receiving from an animal? Sharing its normal stream of consciousness would appear as nightmare with such an enhancement of the senses and such a lack of everyday concepts that the sufferer would be carted off to the nearest asylum. But if the unknown enemy could program a familiar to transmit the Fear and nothing else, that would explain what has been done to me.

88

# July 9

I must now record an incident which I hope is not widely discussed among gossiping horsemen with rumors reaching as far as Penminster. I don't mind being known by close friends as somewhat fey, but I refuse to be saddled with a reputation for the supernatural as if I were some medium in a back room. I can understand why Paddy kept so quiet about all his dealings which were not leatherwork.

To start off my search for the cause of the sending which had nearly destroyed me I decided to take up von Pluwig's offer of a ticket to the International Horse Show and have a longer talk with him. He was most cordial and invited me to watch the events of the last day when he was competing on his famous but not very dependable Arminius for the Puissance. He added that he would enjoy meeting Meg again if it was convenient for me to take her along; he was sure there would be no objection so long as she stayed quiet in my pocket.

I met him for a moment during the intermission and he pressed me to visit the stables half an hour before he entered the collecting ring. I found him in the stall with Arminius and his head groom, watched by a small group of cheery Germans and British who might have been hangers-on or riders in other minor events. He told me that the horse was in top form and had a very good chance of winning if only he didn't trail his off hind. I asked him if that sort of fault was not cured in training by stretching a wire along the top pole so that the horse got a shock if he touched it. No, von Pluwig said, he had never liked the trick and seldom used it with Arminius; my late friend, Paddy Gadsden, had completely cured him, but since Paddy's death the trouble had returned.

I put Meg down on the floor of the stall knowing what she would do, for I had seen her often enough with horses and cattle. She ran around the angles of the stall to get her bearings, cantered over to Arminius's foreleg, smelt the hoof and then stretched up as far as she could. The horse gave a slight start at the prickling of the claws and then put down his noble head in a graceful curve to blow at her. Meg, fearless as ever, threw up her black muzzle in something like a kiss. That was her usual method of investigating the intelligent end of anything on long legs, man or animal, but to anyone who did not know her it was the oddest sight. One could have sworn they were communicating with each other; so they were in a sense, but merely satisfying mutual curiosity.

"Meg, tell him to remember his off hind!" von Pluwig said.

The remark would have sounded humorous to the onlookers. I alone could see that he meant it and I understood why he had turned up at my house out of the blue. He must have had limitless trust in Paddy and Meg, but of course had no idea how the talisman worked. Not even Paddy could charm the horse in such detail. Von Pluwig in the saddle, sensitive body to sensitive body, could do it a hundred times more effectively. Paddy's influence in supervising training was quite a different matter.

I watched the Puissance from my seat. The wall was up to seven feet and only von Pluwig and Felicity Brown were still in. Felicity and Anvil Challenge — both, I expect, desperately tired — knocked down a pole in the treble but cleared the wall as effortlessly as if it were a five-barred gate. Von Pluwig and Arminius flew over the treble but, for the first time, the horse trailed that fatal off hind and dislodged a brick of the wall. A gasp went up

90

from the auditorium, all of course backing the British girl and praying that the brick would fall and that the pair would tie at four faults each. The brick hung there swaying on its point of balance but accountably it did not fall.

After his lap of triumph I went out to see von Pluwig and congratulate him. I noticed several cold looks among the horsemen eddying up and down the alley of the stables. He led me quickly away to the bar and plied me with champagne. I ordered a cold beef sandwich — Meg does not like ham — and slipped her a couple of inches of underdone.

"Meg deserves more," von Pluwig said.

"I don't see why. Arminius did just what he shouldn't."

"I was thinking of the brick."

He was fingering a very full wallet as he paid for the drinks.

"Is there no charity in which you are interested?" he asked.

Only then did it occur to me that he was serious, or at least perplexed about what to make of his luck.

"For God's sake, man!" I exclaimed. "You surely don't believe I had anything to do with it?"

"Of course not! Of course not!" he replied heartily. "What an idea!"

But he shook my hand very warmly and inundated me with invitations to Germany whenever I liked.

Needless to say, Meg and I had nothing whatever to do with the brick remaining at point of balance. Being on von Pluwig's side, I had hoped the brick would not fall but I did not greatly care. In any case telekinesis, the power of the mind to influence inorganic matter, is beyond the shaman, though he is on the right lines in his primitive tendency to consider living and inorganic matter as two aspects of the same thing. If mind could cause a brick to fall, the energy might be derived from such saintly unity with nature that the laws of cause and effect are in suspense. Question: poltergeists? But they do not seem to be under any rational control when they heave bricks about.

Such interference is also beyond the power of mass concentration. There was that vast auditorium praying — if not in so many words — that the brick would fall. The massed appeal had no effect. A comparable case is that of a race meeting where an odds-on favorite is beaten by a head in spite of the condensed petition of the crowd that it should not be.

All this strengthens my theory of how the Robin went to work: through mind to mind, his own obscurely kept in training by the familiar. That Meg could directly influence Arminius is pure superstition. That Paddy needed Meg's actual presence is unlikely since he never took her abroad. So a sort of formula occurs to me. Paddy × Meg can be received by Arminius ÷ von Pluwig. And Alfgif × Meg can be received by bullock. The "magic" does not lend itself to scientific investigation, which is too cerebral and inhibits the sixth sense.

Three inferences may be drawn: (1) the sender of the Fear to Alfgif requires a familiar; (2) he has to be sure that Alfgif is able to receive; (3) a form of the Old Religion still exists in secret and is known to exist not only by the active covens.

So I must play the detective and use cold reasoning. Who could initiate the sending and why? Rule out Bill Freeman, who is all Christian goodness. Rule out George Midwinter; he has a remarkably open mind and genuine curiosity but that is all. Gargary's magic comes out of a syringe. Magistrates, farmers, country businessmen and the Cricket Club are mostly good fellows who have no active receptors and would not have the remotest idea what I mean by them. Nor have I any known enemy in my society unless it's Freddie Newcombe, the seed merchant, whom I, as umpire, gave OUT LBW (which he was) when he was on 99 in the opening match.

Victor Pirrone is somewhat inscrutable, chiefly because of his praiseworthy attempts to appear an English country gentleman when every gesture betrays the Italian. He can have nothing against me; also he is a highly cultured businessman, not a traditional and possibly primitive Sicilian like the priest he mentioned who could make goats dance.

Concha Pirrone, with ancestors happily beyond the reach of government unless government arrives by mule, at least has a familiar which could influence her to open its cage, but that is the limit. She could never program Leyalá to transmit Fear. It would presumably have to be terrified itself, which it isn't. I never knew a more self-confident bird.


## July 14

I have got onto a very promising line. Now that I am not so bound up in my own misery, my mind is not hopelessly subjected to effects but is free to consider causes. Normal thought runs clear and unworried, carrying its moments of inspiration on a healthy stream of trivialities. I am again attending committees that I had missed and discussing local affairs less formally in the saloon bar of the Royal George. I even allowed myself to be persuaded into relinquishing umpiring — that duty of the old and presumably dispassionate — in order to bowl for Penminster, which, after a few hours at the nets to get back a length, I did. A drying pitch was just right for my slow leg-breaks and I took 4 for 20. One of my victims, who had played for Somerset in his time, remarked that nobody but a wizard could make a ball turn like that and play-fully referred to Meg. Now, that's odd and comforting. While haunted by the Fear, I dreaded that I might become known as some sort of eccentric specializing in the occult. Not a bit of it! I'll soon be asked to play tricks at children's parties.

It occurs to me that Men in Black when off duty may have enjoyed the same popularity as a sporting parson. I suspect that the common people in our once merry England took their witches with a sense of humor and were content to let them go to the Devil their own way so long as they were good companions and rumored to bring prosperity.

That is by the way. My promising line is a hunch, nothing so definite as a theory, that the macaw may be in some way a relay station for the curse. I asked Rita to call on Lady Pirrone and to admire the bird. She was to suggest that I ought to be invited to paint it, and she should find out when that godfather from the hills gave it to her and when she brought it to Penminster. I had in fact some intention of painting it, framed by a pediment. Now I will not. It would be adventuring in the dark when I have only the vaguest clue to what I am up against.

Rita must have used all her charm on our plump, unassuming infanta of hills and the sea, who was perhaps flattered by attention from the aristocracy of academe. She brought back the answer that Leyalá had arrived here in the last week of May as a present from her godfather. She said that godfather — whom she referred to only as Uncle Izar — often had given her good advice which she passed on to Victor, who laughed at her — "just like men who

94

don't believe anything" — but often acted on it though he wouldn't admit it. Rita then asked if Uncle Izar was an astrologer. Lady Pirrone seemed rather shocked at the suggestion and said he wasn't, but only very wise and much respected, especially when dealing with land and animals.

"And what do you make of that, my Alfgif?" she asked.

"Izar and his coven?"

"Don't use that coarse northern word! Spain should be all dryads and naiads and Dionysus."

"It isn't Spain. The Basques were there before Celts or Romans, or so Concha tells me. But why should a Basque devil dislike me?"

"Alfgif, make one of your tiger brother guesses at the how, and if you get anywhere near an explanation I'll give you the why. And not till then, because I can't believe it myself."

I did not think that Lady Pirrone was in any way guilty. She simply looked after the familiar and no doubt had detailed instructions from Izar for its care. But the macaw itself is under suspicion since it arrived only a few days before my first attack.

But Leyalá as what I called a transformer station is impossible. Izar at such a distance, far from both the familiar and the target, could not use it for cursing me or any other creature. Yet cursing was an accepted fact in the witch trials. I wish some inquisitive judge had inquired how it was done instead of accepting the familiar as an imp in animal shape which could perform any trick on command.

Training must come in somewhere. Paddy trained Meg. Is it conceivable that Izar programmed the bird's mind by a process of hypnotism? He then presented his macaw computer to Concha Pirrone, where it would be close enough to me to affect me.

But what about identity of target? The macaw cannot be programmed to annoy Alfgif Hollaston, painter, dark-haired, age forty-two, usually dressed in greens and browns, resident at Hollastons. That is ridiculous.

However, the fact of radiation — call it that for want of a better word — is not ridiculous. Take the zebu bull who used to put his head on my shoulder and share my breakfast. What assurance of friendship did he receive from me and offer? What did the birds which used to come to Paddy's hand receive and offer? How does Meg know that a horse will not stamp on her and how does the horse know that the scratching of her claws is not intentional? It appears that there is a radiation of friendship, included by Christ with the Love of God and well known to Saint Francis. The unity of primitive man with his environment is a manifestation of the same thing. I cannot remember a definite example of tiger brother radiating love but he was as skilled as any psychiatrist at taking away fear.

Granted this communication between animals including man, Fear can be received as definitely as Love. Hutchins's bullock was afraid. I did not tell it to be afraid. I merely made it the focus of my will. The effect was to alarm the whole herd. They were afraid because the message was unintelligible, right out of the peaceful pattern of their lives. Anything unintelligible, any powerful signal with no meaning, produces fear in all the higher mammals; for example, dogs are strongly affected by ghosts, whatever ghosts are.

It sounds the very quintessence of the occult to be able to train the macaw as a transmitter; but the only requirement is to hypnotize that amenable bird — and there is nothing very mysterious about that, though the process would be lengthy and the technique must be a dual trance. I myself may well have the gift but not the knowledge. Obviously the thought to be imprinted should be within the capability of the familiar's brain. The macaw, as I wrote sometime back, is intolerably self-confident and of marked personality and would lend itself to some such ecstasy as this: I HUNT. I KILL. I FLY. BE AFRAID. I AM PRESENT.

That last one is a bit doubtful, but animal consciousness must surely include Here and Now.

When I receive the broadcast it suggests to me an unseen, ever-present, hungry carnivore, which is not a carnivore, but a something invisible, fiend or Fury. Tiger brother would have recognized it as the wordless, indescribable thought process of an animal.

That disposes of one difficulty; it is not essential to identify the target. The curse is not like an aimed bullet or a laser beam. It is a short-distance broadcast which will be received wherever it can be received.

Objection! The sending should have affected the highly sensitive Meg but did not. That can be explained. Since she hardly knows what fear is, she is incapable of feeling it. All right, but fear is not the only possible reaction. After a long delay the continued nuisance appeared in Meg as an unaccountable loss of vitality.

If my speculations on the use of the familiar for cursing are anywhere near right, they can be proved.

## July 17

How different from sneaking around to George Midwinter trying to pretend there was nothing wrong with me! I asked him to have a quick lunch at the Royal George between his rounds and his office hours. Over a half-bottle of their best port with our cheese, he opened up on the subject that continued to fascinate him, as I knew he would.

"Have you taught Meg to use a stethoscope yet?" he asked.

I replied that I could easily teach her to hold one if it wasn't too heavy, and added: "I think that my impression that I received her reactions through my fingers was wrong. It's more direct — mind to mind. Did Paddy ever tell you anything of the sort?"

George thought for a bit before answering.

"No. But he did once refer to teaching Meg. I don't know what or how. But since Paddy was quietly doing his stuff before he ever had Meg, it stands to reason that he must have trained her to fit in and be useful."

"Laboratory assistant rather than consulting diagnostician?"

"If you like. But when it comes to registering what you called Meg's temperature readings, mind to mind seems more probable than just tickling her tummy. Friend Meg has definitely got a mind, but don't ask me how Paddy could tap it!"

"Do you yourself ever know what your patients are thinking?"

"If the animal is an intelligent dog or cat, of course I do. But that's observation, not telepathy."

A good vet could not help developing some of the receptors of hunting man, but would not recognize them. So I let it go at that and started a roundabout approach to the evidence I wanted.

"I've a theory, George, that the nervous system of animals is affected by the moon."

"So is ours."

"Especially the first days of June."

"Balls, Alf!"

"Have you never noticed it?"

"No. But I did have a queer case about that time. Gave me the fright of my life! I thought it was rabies."

I led him on. He had been called out to look at a sheep dog. Its owner refused to bring it down to the office and said on the telephone that he had shut it up in a stable and George would see why.

He watched the dog for a time over the stable door. It was slavering at the mouth, suffering from sudden muscular contractions, lying down on its side and only getting up to howl. The farmer said nothing nor did he enter the stable. He caught the dog by the collar with a long shepherd's crook, pulled it within George's reach and nodded.

When George had put the dog down he very carefully lifted the body into the trunk of his car and roared away to the lab in Yeovil for an analysis of the brain and tissues. The lab report was that the dog had been in all-around good health and that the symptoms were unaccountable. They got near to suggesting that George had imagined half of them and had panicked. The farmer didn't blame him, though he had worshiped his sheep dog; it could read their little minds, he said, without any help from him.

I asked George if he remembered the date. Yes, June 5. That was the week when I could stand it no longer and ran away to the Purbeck Hills.

"It had been coming on gradually?"

"Yes. The farmer had been very worried for several days."

It is interesting that the victim should have been a top-class sheep dog of marked sensitivity. "Could read their little minds," the farmer had said. I should have expected that the trouble, if any, would have hit in the wilds. Perhaps it did, but none of us would have known it. I wonder how my vixen is.

"I wish Paddy had been alive," George said as we got up to go. "But I'm not sure that I would have dared to take his advice. How would Meg have reacted, do you think?"

"Much as you. And I doubt if even Paddy could have been certain whether it was rabies or something else attacking the brain."

Poor bloody dog! There but for the grace of God go I.

I did not have to seek out Gargary. He came to me, so brisk and businesslike that I felt he was mentally filing notes for an article in a medical journal. He, Rita and Ginny were the only persons who knew how ill I had been and they rejoiced at my return to normal. Others had only noticed my absence from all my usual resorts and pursuits, ascribing it to an artist's preoccupation with his work.

"And so you are really all right again?" Gargary asked. "It's not just courage?"

"Quite all right."

"And you know the cause?"

"Not unlike the collective fear of a rabbit warren, which you suggested."

"I wasn't serious, Alf, you know. It was you who implied that your phobia was not due to your own subconscious but to an outside agency acting on a sixth sense. What did you do about it? Did you employ any — well — er — technique from Hindu religion?"

"No. I painted it."

"I don't understand."

"I couldn't deal with its form, so I made it formless."

"An abstract?"

"In the sense that it was a picture of emotion, yes."

"Very interesting. They encourage alcoholics to paint pictures. In your case I suppose it's a kind of self-hypnosis?"

"Exactly. You've hit it."

"Would you call prayer self-hypnosis?" he asked.

"Or trance or a unity with the Purpose. Why?"

"Because I seem to have done the right thing without really believing in it."

"Recently?" I asked with as casual an air as I could manage.

"About a month ago."

I got it out of him. At first he very properly suppressed the name of his patient, but it soon became apparent to me that it was Bill Freeman, the one man whose receptors may be as good as my own. He had had a series of terrifying nightmares, dreaming that their two cats had been on his pillow trying to tear his eyes out. The primary cause of the dreams was obvious, Gargary said. The cats had been more impertinent than usual, and one of them had badly bitten Mrs. Freeman.

"It was she who made him come to me," Gargary went on. "They aren't either of them characters to be bothered by bad dreams, but I have a feeling that Mrs. Freeman resented the insult to her cats. She is very fond of them in spite of the civil war that goes on. Well, I asked the usual questions and tried the usual remedies, but the dreams continued and Freeman's imagination turned the cats into imps from hell, after him even when he was awake. He's a bit of a religious maniac, you know.

"I couldn't do much more about it, short of sending him to a psychiatrist, which somehow seemed to me all wrong for Bill, so I told him to confide in the vicar. He said the vicar didn't approve of him. Bloody old fool — the vicar, I mean! There he had an earnest Christian performing minor miracles in his parish and he didn't approve of him! But in the end he seems to have done his duty, whatever it was, and it worked."

I remembered at once Bill Freeman's obscure remark when he implied that he had been cured of some sickness of the mind by a minister of religion.

"And the cats?" I asked.

"Cleared out for a week's hunting on their own, I understand, and returned in a better temper. They tried to apologize by coming home with a fine young rabbit, but rather spoilt the effect by depositing it on Mrs. Freeman's freshly laundered sheet."

How it all fits in! Imagine a village three or four hundred years ago where the inhabitants, though agriculturalists, still retained vestiges of their ancestors' beliefs and sensitivities to nature! Suddenly animals start behaving strangely and there are cases of psychosomatic illness, some of them ending in death. The known and suspected witches, up to then tolerated for their healing powers but distrusted, immediately become the objects of collective hysteria and are jailed until herded to the assizes to be hanged, imprisoned or acquitted, while their Robin, heartbroken but helpless, finds business abroad.

I suspect that the vicar does not know how to use exorcism — always assuming that it's effective against a curse — but as a man of undoubted faith and simplicity merely prayed with Bill Freeman. There we come into realms of the spirit which Paddy would have understood without words, but I am frustrated and seek for parallels.

Just as the communal praise and the dancing and feasts of animism have power to heal body and mind but appear mere playacting to most of us, so the solemn ritual of the Church would seem melancholy to our far ancestors in the forest; yet both offer the same access to the Purpose as my own prayer offered in painting. An apparently "evil" influence — if it is fair to call Izar and the macaw evil when I have only the vaguest idea of the mechanics and none of the motive — is defeated by the contemplation of unity. Because I can rarely find the beauties of primitive paganism in Christianity, I doubt if anything less than the full hosannas of a cathedral service could have helped me. My own Job-like faith, persisting through the agony, did.

I am reminded that one night my brother, standing with me on a barren outcrop of rock above the trees of the jungle, asked if I knew what the stars were singing to us. I replied that I heard but it was beyond my understanding, and I translated for him — since the marvel of the words went easily into Munda and perhaps into any of man's languages: "When the morning stars sang together, and all the sons of God shouted for joy."

Far away a tiger roared, and he said: "So does our brother shout, Alf, but we may only shout in the silence of our hearts."


## July 21

Ginny has been bothered by the police again. I thought that we had heard the last of Paddy's death and that they had merely added it to their list of unsolved crimes. They accepted the fact that she would be asleep when my stolen car was returned but were still not happy about the earlier time when it was driven away, which, they had decided, was around about eleven.

She had brought this on herself by saying at the first investigation — trying to cut corners out of loyalty — that of course she always heard me from her apartment in the stable block if I drove away in the evening after dinner.

The police had proved by experiment that this was not true. She could not hear a car started up in the drive if she was in her apartment. Very intelligently they now wanted to find out who, besides myself, could be quite certain that she would have gone home to the apartment by eleven. It was a vague question, difficult to answer since I seldom entertained at home. Ginny tells me that she could not think of anyone who would be sure except Paddy, with whom I sometimes talked late, in summer usually sitting in the garden or strolling under the trees. She also mentioned Miss Vernon, adding for the sake of propriety that Miss Vernon only called on business when she would be sure to find me in.

She thought this renewed interest plain silly, but I can see what the police are after. They are still wondering if I lent my car to someone and whether I told the loyal Ginny to pay no attention if she were still in the house and heard the car driven away while I was at the Pirrone party.

Then the superintendent had the damned impertinence to call on Rita and inquire — with infinite tact and circumlocution — if she could tell him anything of Ginny's routine. She replied, no doubt with a touch of courteous hauteur, that she was not conversant with my domestic arrangements, but so far as she knew Ginny prepared a simple supper for me when I was in, washed up and returned to her apartment.

This I learned when I ran into her on the street and dragged her off for a drink in the Royal George. She insisted on taking me home to her cottage for lunch, tempting me — my God, does she think she needs to? — with an offer of cold guinea fowl in aspic. That, with a bottle of

Meursault between us, was too delicate and blue-skied a meal for a conversation which would have been better fitted to the bloody foreleg of a half-grilled deer and the drip from unseen trees hissing on the fire.

"I think they have let you off lightly," she said. "Your story was suspect from the start. Whoever arranged to take your car knew that Ginny was most unlikely to hear it go off and return, knew your habit of going to Penminster parties on foot and knew that you would have a perfect alibi. Alfgif, who could be sure of all that but you? So from the police point of view it's ten to one that you lent your car to someone without knowing why it was wanted, and afterwards you won't say who it was for reasons of friendship and because you are convinced that Paddy's death was pure accident."

I told her if the police thought that, they were crazy. I wouldn't protect Paddy's murderer for a moment. And it was murder, not an accident.

"It hasn't occurred to you that it could be suicide?"

Yes, it had occurred to me and to everyone else, all of us mystified as to why Paddy did not move out of the way when he must have heard or seen the car. But there were no conceivable motives for suicide, financial, emotional or from fear of incurable disease.

Rita filled my glass and changed the subject, reminding me that after she had given me her report on Concha Pirrone and the macaw we had agreed that the unknown Izar could be responsible for my haunting and she had promised to give me a why if I could give her a how.

"Now can you?" she asked.

I have never been able to pigeonhole Rita's beliefs. And what do they matter anyway? My love of her is strong enough to welcome and include them all. She takes clairvoyance and telepathy as proven and I believe she pays for a horoscope, yet she fails to see that every faith must present its true meaning in the form of myth, and that "myth" is not a term of abuse. Religion to her is a human curiosity, like ambition, which moves history and is therefore of vital importance. That historical standpoint is useful because, myth or not, she keeps an open mind wherever there is firsthand evidence.

So I started off with a memory of tiger brother, who kept, fed and enjoyed the company of a large, tame toad. He told me it was not a toad; it was a snake to frighten away leopards and hyenas. Tigers, being of our clan and friendly, had no need to be thus frightened. At the time and up to recently I took this as a bit of hocus-pocus. I remember writing that tiger brother had no familiar, but now I see how toad fits into the unity. Shaman hypnotizes toad. Toad emanates the snake warning — which exists, all right, if you can feel it — and intruder thinks better of entering hut. Shaman's direct command to the leopard or hyena is not impossible, but he might not be present. The toad-snake, however, always remains in the hut.

"Wearing a precious jewel in his head!" she remarked.

"Exactly. I wonder if Shakespeare had learned from some admiring Robin that there was a reality behind the myth."

That was my prelude to the use of Leyalá and I went on to tell Rita of the experiences of Gargary and Midwinter which seemed to prove my theory.

"And the creature which is the medium is itself unaffected?" she asked.

"Yes. Think of that network of brain cells as a computer programmed by the shaman. And you don't expect a computer to get up and run."

"Well, if it's a computer you have only to pull out the plug. Kill the macaw!"

"Not now that I have won."

"*If* you have won."

I said, perhaps too boldly, that I would cross that bridge when I came to it and that now she must tell me what Izar — if it was Izar — had against me.

"You know the anthropologists' theory of the king who must die for the people?" she asked.

"Yes. And I've spotted remnants of the belief here and there in India."

"And did you know that was why William Rufus was killed?"

I did not, having only learned the schoolbook verdict that he was a "bad" king. She explained to me how historians had been puzzled by all the abuse poured on him by monastic chroniclers when the rest of the evidence showed that he was brave, just, chivalrous and accepted with love by the English who hated his father, the Conqueror. Why did the common people follow his bier from the New Forest to Winchester? Why was it said that all the way his blood dripped to the earth? And why when Walter Tyrell hesitated to shoot, did he cry: "Draw, draw your bow for the Devil's sake and let fly your arrow or you will be sorry for it!"? And why was his death expected and foretold all over Europe?

"He was the King and Grand Master, the grandson of Robert the Devil. That's the explanation. Churchmen knew him for what he was and were appalled by his contempt for them; but the mass of the Saxons, who were as much pagan as Christian, adored him for living for them and dying for their land. This isn't a lecture, Alfgif, so I'll just give you Rufus. There's a good case too for Henry II as Grand Master and a better one for Gilles de Rais, who was Joan of Arc's commander in the field."

I presumed that she knew her stuff and I saw the implications, but I said I could not for a moment believe that the gentle Paddy was the secret shaman of Western Europe.

"Ah, but the Grand Master did not have to die. If he could find a willing victim to die in his place he had another seven years."

"You're suggesting that the rite still exists in the Europe of today?"

"There must be more people than you, Alfgif, who share the vision that all living creatures are one within what you call the Purpose. Their myths and forms of worship may be as odd as tiger brother's. And that's no odder than some of those American sects. I told you I couldn't really believe it, but the evidence keeps piling up. And you must admit that your Paddy was a Man in Black."

"He had no coven."

"Of course he hadn't. A village coven would be an absurdity in these days when one can fly to Paris in the time that it took to ride from Penminster to Wincanton. So couldn't a coven now be international? Remember all the strangers and foreigners who came to his funeral!"

That I had explained by his reputation among horsemen, but it had always puzzled me. So did the fact that a saddler in a little country town had executors of international standing. And if Rita was right, where did I come in? That I did come in somewhere was certain.

"Why do you think he gave me Meg?"

"Because he saw you were a kindred spirit just as your tiger brother did. And perhaps because it was a mark of honor and good for Meg and perhaps because you are loved. Will you start a coven, my Robin, and dance with me on our downs in moonlight?"

I replied that I was no good at dancing — my coldness

breaking my heart — and pretended to be impatient to hear why, according to her, I was considered an enemy.

She said that Paddy's plan had gone wrong. He reckoned that the car which was to kill him could never be identified. But it was identified, and what should have been just another hit-and-run accident threatened to end up in Penminster magistrates' court, where I, to protect myself from the allegation of having lent my car, might have talked.

"They didn't know how much you could guess or what Paddy might have told you. What they did know was that you were half pagan, half Christian — a free-lance witch, as you once called it. Now suppose an outwardly sane, responsible citizen like you got some outstanding authority — anthropologist or historian — to give evidence of the former rites of the witch religion; then the police would gasp but investigate the movements of anyone staying with the Pirrones on the night of the party. And worst of all the popular papers would have witchcraft right across the front page. Half a joke, of course, but secrecy would be compromised. And there might be an arrest.

"So anything you say must be discredited. That's where Leyalá comes in. You take your unbelievable nonsense to solid Somerset police. Gargary says with regret that you are mentally unbalanced. All your friends agree that you have been avoiding them and behaving oddly. George Midwinter, Ginny and even I would admit, putting it politely, that you needed a holiday" — her tone sounded irritable but I deserved it, "— so Mr. Hollaston would be encouraged to spend a short period with the headshrinkers at a funny-farm to cure his imagination, and when he came out he would find an unsquashable rumor that he killed Paddy himself while of unsound mind. And how's that?"

# VI

## July 25

It's all now quite clear. At the weekend I called up
Lady Pirrone and asked if I might come over and renew
my acquaintance with Leyalá. The Pirrones were both
most cordial. Sir Victor opened a bottle of some dark
Sicilian wine, still glowing with the past warmth of lava,
and asked for my opinion. My opinion is worthless — for
who am I to pick and choose among nectars? — but my
enthusiasm most Latinly delighted him. I am certain that
both of them are entirely innocent. Concha Pirrone is a

very pious Catholic, and while she knows that her god-father is a man of mysterious insight and reliable hunches she would never dream that he, as she would put it, had sold his soul to the Devil.

The bird recognized me without a doubt, his chuckling in no way inspired by the trouble he had involuntarily caused me but rather by the moment of communion which we had shared. When confidence all around had been established, I asked Sir Victor why he had chosen to live at Penminster.

"Oh, my wife saw a photograph of it in *Country Life* and fell in love," he said. "And it suits me as well as another — the house not too big; the garden beautiful, though I miss my cypresses. And it's ideal for weekend visitors if they come from the Mediterranean and want to understand what it is that the English so love about their land. I would have liked to be nearer London, but we use the port less and less and here I am handy to Bristol and Southampton."

"Izar promised to send you some cypresses from Granada," Lady Pirrone interrupted.

"That's your godfather who gave you Leyalá?" I asked. "I think he may be the oldish man, remarkably tough, who was talking to me at your housewarming party."

"That sounds like him. But then it was so sad. He was taken ill and had to go to bed."

I had no idea whether I had seen Uncle Izar or not. But the shot in the dark had produced a marvelous and un-expected lead.

Next day, feeling like a private eye and faintly ashamed of it, I decided to call on Bastard, Broome and Bastard, our local estate agents, who handled the sale of the Manor House. I enjoy old Bastard. He is immensely proud of his surname, which was invented by Charles II and the Earl of Rochester in the course of one of their drunken evenings when they called for Rochester's baby son, who till then had been hidden under the voluminous skirts of the Duchess of Cleveland's favorite waiting woman, presented him with his surname and, to make up for the insult, the coat of arms which faces the visitor behind Bastard's desk.

He never seems busy outside his auctions and got in first with his questions. How was Miss Vernon getting on down the valley? He supposed I saw something of her. He was very well aware that, if I did, nobody would be any the wiser, so his pleasantly dirty mind sensed the opportunities. I headed him off by saying that I believed the Water Board was insisting on charging her a water rate though she drew it from her own well. That got him fulminating about local goverment in general, and I was able to mention that Pirrone had told me his rates were outrageous.

"It takes a wealthy man to be really angry over a few quid," he said. "So I hope he gives them hell."

"I'm always surprised that he bought the place."

"It was ready to walk into, you see. All redecorated a couple of years ago, and just the job to appeal to a foreigner who doesn't want trouble with builders, surveyors and planning permission."

I said that Sir Victor was a valuable import and wouldn't like to be called a foreigner.

"Well, he is, ain't he? But I was thinking of others who showed interest. One old boy got onto it before we had even advertised the place for sale."

"The usual Arab?"

"Not down here in Somerset! No, some kind of Spaniard. I wouldn't be surprised if he recommended it to the Pirrones."

"I think he was at the Pirrone party. I wish I could remember his name."

"We must have it somewhere. He told me that he was interested in Dorset Horns and wanted to hear of any prize rams to be sold privately."

A clerk in the downstairs office easily found the name for him. The inquirer was a Mr. Izar Odolaga with the address of a London bank. His visit had been in the last week of January. That left plenty of time for the sale to go through and for the Pirrones to move in before that fatal May 12.

When I escaped from the geniality of old Bastard — he would have been distressed to know in what a mood — I did not go home immediately. I walked away from Penminster through the wearisome sanity of council houses and market gardens and the sewage farm where my stream had entered the culture zone and been put to work, at last taking refuge in the woodland at the foot of the downs after wandering up the valley and passing above Rita's cottage. I did not want to see her. Mourning for my dear, incomprehensible Paddy, I did not want to see anyone. Everything had fallen into place confirming the slaughter of Paddy by this Izar Odolaga. One had only to start with the reasonable assumption that the Pirrones really did want a country house.

I saw the sequence of events as something like this: Odolaga, visiting Paddy, learns that the manor is for sale. Paddy himself may have suggested the setup if he had already agreed to the sacrifice — a cold thought which made me shiver. Odolaga then steers his goddaughter towards the house, drawing her attention to a photograph of the place. She inspects it and he assures her that it is ideal and will bring the Pirrones luck. Sir Victor shrugs his shoulders; if she wants the house, it will do.

Once the manor is bought and the housewarming party arranged, Paddy directs the plot: the Pidge, my car, the absolute certainty that I will not be using it and will have an unbreakable alibi if anything goes wrong. Odolaga handles the Pirrone end. Obviously he must be a house-guest at the time of the party and must be able to be absent for a few hours without anyone knowing. How he managed it was unimportant. I could never know on what excuse he locked his bedroom door or was able to choose a room with access to the garden.

Below me, not far away, was my vixen's earth, and I looked to her for comfort — not that I expected to see her at midday, but the scent and signs of her would tell me that she at least was fulfilling herself within our common world. I padded as gently as she over last year's leaves and looked down on the chalk-flecked terrace at the mouth of the earth. The cubs had left, though they should still have been learning to hunt with mother; neither had she herself been home for some time. All this I knew partly by faintness of scent, partly by dust in the tracks, partly by a silence beyond the silence to be detected by the ears. As I went down towards the stream, my eye was caught by the remains of a recent kill among tufts of trampled grass. I thought at first it was a lamb and then saw that the skull was hers. The smallest bones had been scattered and cracked; the larger, which she would have broken, only showed the gnawings of ineffectual teeth. She had died in the open and her hungry cubs had eaten her, a victim serving her purpose to the last. My mind finds some indefinable parallel with Paddy. Him I cannot re-venge because I do not understand the meaning or the worth of his sacrifice. But I now know who is responsible for the end of my vixen, dying of the madness which was intended for me.

## August 1

The black night of the soul. That is what the Christian mystics called it. Tiger brother would have spoken of the capture of the soul. As so often, saint and shaman both mean the same. It has nothing to do with the Fear. I could bear that. At least I was vividly alive like any terrified creature. Now for over a week I have been dead and empty. I cannot even paint. What I believed to be power turns out to be only obscurity. There is no doubt that what I used to call my picture postcards are of more value.

It is Paddy's sacrifice which depresses me. One can only take it as a lunatic rite of a lunatic cult. My saintly Paddy, keeping his religion to himself yet spreading far and wide his own goodness, can be compared with the pastor of some primitive Christian sect who also radiates love and righteousness but imagines his God as human and angry: a half-god disapproving the marvelous mechanism of life — the flesh, as the pastor would call it — which may on no account be worshiped through senses made for worship.

All my reverence is challenged. Meg represents joy in the Purpose rather better than any bishop. On the other hand the bishop represents the suffering of man rather better than Meg.

And whose life could Paddy have considered so valuable to Megs and bishops that it ought to be extended? It could not be Izar Odolaga's life. That's certain. Paddy would have recognized evil in him, the abuse of power. Then who? Anyone from a village priest to a microbiologist, each performing miracles in his own way. Of the two, the priest seems more likely; his miracles would so easily restore faith and awe. And yet suppose the man behind the electron microscope were on the verge of manipulating the nervous system of the brain to prove and analyze the action of mind at a distance?

What nonsense! Who the hell is worth the sacrifice?

Black night of the soul, yes! I am like Meg when she felt some effect of Leyalá's transmission and could no longer play. All passion spent. Why do I bother with Rita? Love is an inconvenience like any other, almost a curse in itself.

I might as well be a gentle, unworried animal like Concha Pirrone, satisfied within her own fat. Not fair! At least she can pray. I cannot. There have been times when I could repeat the Lord's Prayer, concentrating almost with tears upon the full meaning of the words or such meaning as I chose to put upon them.

There is no unity for me with the Purpose and it is not within the Purpose that there should be. I shall paint my picture postcards and be the jolly artist in the company of genial fools like Bastard and the rest. Such an easy fellow, they'll say, after his little illness. Must have done him good.

Bastard. A reminder. In Penminster last Wednesday I saw his red waistcoat bearing down on me like the unavoidable clown in a circus.

"I had that sturdy old Spanish fellow in my office the day before yesterday," he said. "I put him on to a ram down Blandford way if he likes to pay the price."

I had no need to ask where he was staying. That is his second visit to the Pirrones. The first was to murder Paddy. I wonder what this second was for.

"He asked after you," Bastard added. "I told him that we had not seen so much of you as we liked. Always shut away painting hard, ha, ha! But now you were back in good form."

Odolaga would have known that already. He might have suffered some kind of rebound from his devilry with the macaw. Tiger brother used to hint that there were dangers for a shaman if his magic were absorbed by more powerful magic. But there is no necessity for any such mystification. If he exchanges correspondence with his goddaughter and encourages her to amuse him with local gossip he'd have a dozen pages of waffle in her spidery, nunnery writing, complete with exclamation marks.

It is tempting to imagine that he could be responsible for my depression, but I do not believe it. I am suffering from disgust and reaction after discovering the cruelty and worthlessness of all this misuse of spiritual energy by Paddy, by Odolaga and by me. I need tiger brother to dance himself unconscious and bring back my soul from its underworld.

How many other religious follies, I wonder, have been resurrected to drift like lost spirits through our Western society? I have come upon a whole school of unsuspected practitioners: that quiet saddler in a country town; a Basque farmer; a likely nest of Sicilians more secret than the Mafia; von Pluwig and his superstitious circle who believe without knowing what they believe; the strangers at Paddy's funeral. And on the edge of them there must be others like myself, able to heal and transmit thought with or without the aid of a familiar, who respect the holiness of a gift which needs no barbaric ritual.


## August 7

Gargary has been here to ask me if I would care to lend Ginny to Rita for a day or two. Meg and I could send to the zoo for some monkeys, he said, and roast them on a stick. Yes, he could get in a daily woman from Penminster, but the presence of a stranger might only get on Rita's nerves and add to her exasperation. She was not bothering to cook for herself, and the cottage seemed to him just a scrapyard of dirty glasses, of books lying wherever she had read them and paper littering the floor around the wastepaper basket.

I asked in alarm if she had called him in and why. No, there was nothing physically wrong with her. She had turned up at his office to demand whatever he had which was the opposite of a tranquilizer. It was a curious request and she would not elaborate on it. Office hours were over and so, on a sound medical instinct that he might learn more from watching than listening, he had driven her back to her cottage, where the signs of withdrawal had disturbed him. She did burst out once, saying that she hated the cottage and its loneliness and longed for the term to begin. When he replied that nothing stopped her from returning to Oxford immediately, she said she wasn't going to run away just because she couldn't get on with her work.

It's nearly a week since I saw her. She was sitting on the bank of the stream, where two green terraces form an angle and a soft back, with a writing pad and three books, none of them open, and seemed to have been following some intense flow of thought, since she started when I called to her. She was rather silent and at first I supposed that I had interrupted her at some point where a synthesis of her reading had formed in her mind. Then I wondered if Meg and I could have hurt her by some lack of tact over which women are inclined to brood while the offender remains blankly ignorant.

Meg took a long look at her before we went on our way. I can read Meg's reaction to depression or neurosis more certainly than her recognition of physical pain, but it is always hard to distinguish between emanations from her and from myself; so I discounted Meg's diagnosis of melancholy, assuming that I myself was saddened by my useless devotion to Rita and that Meg had caught my sense of inadequacy.

I went over to the cottage with Ginny, pretending that it was just a friendly call. When Ginny saw Rita's eyes and the general mess — how different from the scented day when I had lunched there! — she exclaimed that she was going to stay and clean up until dear Miss Vernon could get somebody else, and meanwhile she was sure that Mr. Alfgif wouldn't mind. She played her part brilliantly, shooing me away and filling the place with her calm and sweetness.

Only a fortnight ago I boasted to Rita that I had won; and she, seeing more clearly than I the dangers of this primeval cult into which I have blundered, answered: *if you have won*. I suspect that I have not, though Rita should be as invulnerable to a curse as any politician. She is a highly civilized, urban woman with none of the hunting receptors. I myself can be persecuted by a competent shaman. She, I should have thought, could not. And yet ... and yet over and over again in the witch trials of England and in the present practice of African witch doctors one comes across the sending of this singular apathy which ends in death.

How perfect an object for retribution, if that is what Odolaga wants! But can he know how important she is to me? I must find out what really brought him here again. Concha Pirrone, who entertains no suspicions, may be able to give me a lead. She said that she wanted to meet the famous Meg again and be shown my funny, square English house and its garden.

## August 10

I asked her to tea. When the chauffeur opened the door of the car for her she waddled imposingly out, looking like an overfed Spanish princess in mourning, and greeted me with just the proper convent-trained graciousness. She became almost flirtatious as I took her across the lawn into hidden corners where old Walter, whose taste is for miniature effects, had imposed discipline. Her visit wasn't very correct, was it? Giggle, giggle. But she was sure that Victor wouldn't mind if — giggle, giggle — Miss Vernon did not. She looked up at me with her head on one side waiting for crumbs. I replied that Miss Vernon's interests ran to six hundred pages with footnotes, and added "unfortunately" to avoid the impression that I found Rita tedious — too gross a lie to be believed.

On so English a day, with wind lazily moving clouds in the upper atmosphere and the air motionless over the ground, tea in the garden was traditional, but I doubted if I had a chair that would hold her. The tough, ancestral canvas of my father's deck chairs was showing signs of age and she could not possibly fit between the iron arms of the white-painted garden seats. There was no Ginny to solve the problem so I had embellished the curved stone bench in the bower of the too straggly rose garden with gay cushions and laid the tea table opposite with Meg in attendance.

Too straggly! How could I have written that? I find in myself a neat desire to clean it up and commit a ladylike watercolor. To hell with this passivity! All my home and its valley used to be my garden. Have the forests of tiger brother, so rich with life, clean gone from my blood? And who painted my *Holy Well* and *Columns of the Sun*?

Meg, after investigating the delicate feet (being born an Odolaga, Concha had no fear of her), decided that the rest was too ponderous and humped away with a slice of cake, from which she extracted the almonds and currants, leaving the remainder for the birds. Undoubtedly bait, not charity.

I did not have to introduce the subject of Uncle Izar. Prattling sweetly about empty incidents of an empty week, she did it herself, telling me that Victor had brought him down from London for the night and they had had such fun. They had been talking after dinner about hypnotism and things — Odolaga of course leading the conversation warily towards the "things" — and Victor had said it was all nonsense and got up to open another bottle, which he always did when people talked about what he did not want to understand. And then Uncle Izar said he would show him and he hypnotized poor Leyalá, who gave a squawk and fell off his perch. She told him he was very naughty and he was to put her lovely back at once, so he waved his hands and Leyalá got right up and didn't seem to know what had happened to him.

So far I had two interesting revelations: the debriefing of Leyalá and the fact that Concha was sure to have gossiped about the suspected idyll between the two lonely neighbors far apart from each other but joined together by the clear water and the woods.

She told me that Uncle Izar could heal. Yes, really! She remembered that when she was a little girl she had fallen down and cut her cheek open and he had stopped the bleeding. Well, somebody had to know how to cure up there in the valleys where until recently, if medical attention were needed, patient or doctor had to ride or walk.

This gave me an opening. I dared not ask for Odolaga's

address in case he heard I had done so and guessed why, so I asked what sort of country was that of her mother's family.

"Oh, it's so hard to explain," she said. "It's between two main roads to France and though it's in Spain it's easier to reach from France. Terrible, fierce country but so very green and beautiful."

"And doesn't Victor believe that Mr. Odolaga can heal?" I asked.

Her artless babble of a reply was so packed with information that I must try to remember her own words and put them down for future reference.

"He says he doesn't. He says he has had enough of that sort of thing from ignorant peasants in Sicily. But Uncle Izar is quite different. He's wonderful. When Victor first came to Bilbao he fell off the dry dock and had a concussion and afterwards a sort of stroke and couldn't move his fingers on one hand. The doctors said it would be very long before he was well. So my mother sent for Izar — he's her first cousin, you see — and in a week Victor could hold a pen again and write.

"Well, we were both so fond of each other already, but my father wouldn't hear of me marrying a Sicilian. He thought Sicilians were horrible people, all bandits and gangsters. But Izar kept on insisting that Victor was the right man for me and he went to Sicily himself to meet the family. And when he came back he said that they too had a mountain estate and we had a lot in common with them. My father declared that he couldn't see that the Odolagas and the Pirrones had anything in common except that they had no bathrooms and kept sheep. But my mother and Izar got their own way and we were married."

It's sticking out a mile what the Pirrones and Odolagas had in common. And I have more understanding of Victor. In spite of the best proof of faith healing he could possibly want, he won't face it. He may resemble my father, who had not inherited the Alfgif faculties, showed no interest, wouldn't let himself believe and brought me up with no information beyond the most prosaic family history. Like him, Victor avoids the inexplicable. He knows a lot — I remember Rita saying that he was a rich source of footnotes — but dismisses it all as peasant superstition. I wonder if it has occurred to him to question his astonishing luck in material matters.

Myself I know nothing of luck, nor, I think, did tiger brother, though naturally he took credit for any stroke of luck that came the way of the clan. The conversation between Paddy and George Midwinter at the races is the only intimation I have that luck can be influenced. After saying that he would never use his gift to make money, Paddy added that if anything could make two liquids in the same glass remain separate when mixed it would be the interference of mind. He also made the odd remark that one could be director of a brewery without knowing how to pull a pint. Did that mean that he was aware of certain specialities of Robins but he himself did not or could not practice them? However that may be, he could bring luck to his friends without pulling any mysterious pints, as he brought to me when he sent around Molay, that stately Levantine customer of his who bought and did not buy the *Holy Well*. I wonder what his relations with Paddy were. At the time I had no reason for present curiosity.

I parted from Concha Pirrone on affectionate terms. I like the woman and her gentle face. It is no fault of hers that her godfather is a murderer and as vicious a witch as ever deserved hanging. I could forgive him for what he did to me. I would at least listen to his dogma of why

Paddy had to die. But his attack on Rita cries out for action and revenge.

Revenge. I don't really mean that. Revenge is pointless. What I do mean is: Stop It Or Else! But what "or else"? A miserable Robin I should make! I do not know enough to protect her. I merely guess at the realities of a tradition which Paddy and great-great-grandfather preserved. I'd give this Uncle Izar a sending of all the imps in hell if I could call them up — assuming of course that the illusion would frighten him.

Frighten him. There's the germ of an idea. I can remember tiger brother laughing with some embarrassment when I once accused him of descending to conjuring tricks. He replied that the power had left him, and it was understood between us — without coarsely referring to it in so many words — that his dependent clans must not be tempted to present him with second-rate cuts of monkey because he was giving a second-rate service. Conjuring tricks, yes. A betrayal but pardonable. When a priest, as must sometimes happen, finds that his faith is overwhelmed by flat and empty reasoning he does not black out the altar and take a cut in salary. Routine supports him till meaning returns to prayer.

Odolaga is probably afraid of me as rather more than an awkward witness in court. There is the behavior and failure of Leyalá to be considered. There is Paddy's gift of his familiar. There is the rumor of esoteric knowledge picked up by me in India. If any sinister and unaccountable disaster were to strike him, his guilty conscience could very well jump at the so-called occult for an explanation rather than a tiger brother fraud.

Malevolence, I am sure, can be carried by the adept to the target through direct transmission or by way of the familiar. It may or may not have been the cause of that fool spraining his ankle when he distracted me as I was near to painting the *Columns of the Sun*. But there are simpler methods that I have learned from hunting man. If by close observation the shaman works out beforehand the probable course of his human prey, he can set a trap — perhaps material, perhaps subjective, but always inscrutable — and afterwards can publicize his triumph as due to the excellent intelligence reports he is continually receiving from the ancestral spirits.

However, no shaman could preserve his secrets on the open downs of Wessex. More opportunities are offered by the country where Odolaga lives. Concha described it as terrible and fierce but beautiful, and Sir Victor had said something of precipices and pastures. All I had in the house was a copy of *The Song of Roland* in Norman French and modern French which Rita lent me — an eight-hundred-year-old authority, but the minstrel could not have gone far wrong on the general topography.

*High are the mountains, high and huge and shadowed,*
*The valleys deep, their waters running fast.*

That impulsive translation misses the melancholy refrain of the Norman French but tells of country where I should be at home — allowing for more clothes than the loincloth I wore among the Birhors — so long as the forests are still there. "Tenebrus" must refer, I think, to trees as well as the north face of gorges. There may be language trouble, but so near the frontier French should carry me through. The real difficulty will be to keep the close presence of a stranger hidden from Odolaga.

# VII

## August 16

This journal has become more than a habit. Started as an attempt to analyze the sending and thus preserve my sanity, I keep it up for reference in case the unknowables of malice and geography become instant, sinister beyond my comprehension and demanding.

I am writing this at dawn of what should be the final day. I have made myself comfortable as any expectant carnivore, at the edge of the tree line where I have only to crawl up a little to watch and consider my objective. All senses are awake as they have not been since dawn in the hills of the Deccan and most certainly were not when I left Penminster in a state of stagnant apathy only relieved by anger.

So far as Penminster is concerned, I have gone to Paris to see an old friend in the Embassy of India. George Midwinter has taken Meg, and I can imagine him surreptitiously trying to prove a value in which he half believes; in any case they understand each other. Rita remained impenetrable, only saying a little formally that she hoped I had not decided to go away because I had lent her Ginny.

I must admit I am pleased with myself. Even tiger brother would have found it hard to slip through such country and remain unseen except as a distant figure on the high pastures. My object has been to remain a ghost while in Odolaga's homeland. I intend to leave no shred of evidence for the Civil Guard and yet to allow Uncle Izar to suspect, when the time comes for it, that I might be responsible for whatever damage a ghost can do.

I crossed the Pyrenees from Pau to Huesca to avoid leaving a record of my passage through any of the frontier posts in the Basque country. I then drove west to Pamplona, where I found a lock-up garage in which to park my car. Next morning I took a bus along the road to Bayonne and got off it, still on the Spanish side of the frontier, at what seemed a plausible point for a middle-aged hiker, well tanned and as impermeable as a tortoise, to start exploring the Pyrenees.

I was glad to find that the equipment of present-day youth, so neatly framed to carry on the back, was not as heavy as I expected and that so long as I only had to climb slopes, not rocks, I was easily fit enough to tackle any cross-country route. I brought along half a meter of Pamplona sausage, some bread, fruit, and a liter of brandy to mix with my water. I have no weapons beyond an old and trustworthy hunting knife, a length of whipcord, a handful of goose feathers and a dozen ball-point pens. Nothing in that lot for Customs to suspect.

How long it would take me to run Odolaga to earth I had no idea, for I dared not ask questions and the only pointer was Concha Pirrone's remark that he lived between the two roads to France and was easier to reach from France than from Spain. After leaving the bus on the eastern road, I followed it on foot up to the top of the pass and there sat down to equate what I saw with a small-scale map which was the only one I could find. Eyes and the map agreed. There was blank nothing except green mountain swelling up over green mountain, not a visible village and not a road except donkey tracks disappearing into the valleys. In a sense that eased my problem, for if Odolaga had a profitable estate in the middle of nothing there must be somewhere a wider track by which transport could come and go.

The most likely key to finding him seemed to be a village called Zugarramurdi, which could not be reached without going down the winding pass almost to the frontier and then turning back into the hills. One could say that it was easier to reach from France than Spain. If that was his nearest village, it had to be avoided at all costs but offered an objective for the march. Another pointer — a hint rather than evidence — suggested that I was on ground which the officers of the Inquisition had searched before me. Just before the frontier and close to the road to Zugarramurdi the map showed a tourist attraction called Cave of the Witch. Tradition lingers on where there is so little to disturb it.

Choosing a moment when no one was in sight, I scrambled down to a river on the west of the road and followed it towards France until I came to a tributary rushing down from the broken range where I wanted to be. *The Song of Roland* now came into its own. Though I would not call the mountains high, they gave an impression of massiveness and the valleys were certainly deep with racing water at the bottom. It was slow going, partly because I stuck to the banks of the stream, usually pathless, and partly because here and there the valleys opened out into little meadows even more lovely than the Hollaston paradise where William Hutchins fattens his bullocks — either flowered lawns after the hay harvest or proud with the blades and russet tassels of the maize. Often there was a lonely farmhouse, invisible among the timber till I was on it, and I had to make a silent detour to avoid the smallholder, his dogs and children. During winter it must be impossible to travel far, and hard to communicate with a neighbor.

With an hour of daylight to go and seeing an easy slope to the south, I left the valley and came out on a ridge from which I had a view of the surrounding country. I reckoned that Zugarramurdi was about six miles away as the crow flies and would be much farther for anyone compelled to travel secretly across the grain of the land while depending on compass bearings. I was reminded of old days and roundabout routes forced by torrents and cliffs, where one might not meet another soul in the jungle for a hundred miles. Here my trouble was that I might meet someone around the next bend, unable to avoid his questions and the kindly meant escort to the right path for somewhere I did not want to go. To be seen on a distant skyline did not matter. I watched a party of hikers loaded much as I was and keeping to the high ground. Wherever I could do the same I should arouse no curiosity.

The key to the country seemed to be a steep cone well

to the west of Zugarramurdi and close to the line of the frontier. It was quite unlike the other hills, the base and sides covered with dark forest and the top bare so that it resembled a volcano where streams of green lava had poured down over black rock. I chose it as my first objective and made good time to the foot of the peak since most of the way was over high pastures. In the lingering dusk I climbed up some eight hundred feet by way of a ravine where the snow water had washed away most of the dense cover of brush and bramble leaving a stony passage through pools and over shelves of rock. When I came to a slender waterfall I camped beside it. However long I spend on this punitive expedition, the half meter of Pamplona sausage will see me through. Marvelously concentrated stuff! And I need not have carried fruit. The first blackberries are ripe.

I woke just before dawn, unable to throw off a dream that I was within some vast Presence, swallowed as by a giant. The mountain was surrounded by its own dawn like its own dark rock and foliage: an even ring of cloud below the pale sky. At sunrise this private cloud retired into the hollows of the cone by wisps and layers, formless shapes but so dense that I could have made a wash portrait of them.

I continued the ascent as far as the beginning of the grass. It was a haunted but most convenient peak, for I could scramble most of the way around it in low cover, only climbing up to the open when my line of sight had to clear the tops of forest trees. To the east were the grander Pyrenees, rising and falling like ocean swell and throwing up plumes of rock where tranquillity was shattered. Down a valley to the north was a glimpse of France; on the west the cone became more of a ridge, descending to a plateau broken by narrow, wooded val-

behind. It seemed likely that he was bound for the plateau to run his eyes over his sheep, so I returned on my route to the head of the valley, now sure that it was safe, and stealthily made my way up the edge of the plateau, leaving my awkward pack behind me in the woods.

This plain of rich, rough grass was bare of any sort of cover and sloped gently down to a valley on the north containing the amphitheater where I had seen a herd of cattle. As there was no sign of Odolaga, I assumed he was down among the cows. Meanwhile I was in the only possible place for observation.

After an hour or so Odolaga rode up from the north, and by his side trotted the most handsome and vigorous billy goat I have ever seen: a magnifico of goats. It was pure black, with short, dainty horns above the forehead curls, and in the prime of life. Odolaga dismounted, throwing the reins on the horse's neck and letting it loose to graze. Before doing so it first nuzzled the goat and rested its head for a moment on the black neck.

Odolaga joined the pair, caressing both of them. He then walked off a little way and challenged the goat to butt his outstretched palms. It went for him, reducing speed just in time to slam forehead harmlessly into hands, and rose on hind legs with forelegs on his shoulders. I knew from the experience of my own familiar what the pair were expressing to each other, and I would have let myself surrender to the common joy if I had not also remembered why I was there and perceived to what precious object I must direct my sending.

As they came nearer, the low sun was full on Odolaga's face. It was massive and round but not fat, and topped by an unmanageable mass of gray hair. The gray eyes, in that light with a touch of green, were far apart and exceptionally large. Under the circumstances my impression of him had to be more charitable than the first distant examination inspired by hatred.

After the play he rode off, leaving the black goat among the flock with a final caress. Dusk was now falling. I returned to my pack and ate and dozed a little till the moon should rise and give me enough light in that clear air to make a circuit of the plateau. In the heavy blue-black of twilight the Presence again threatened, created perhaps by the spent energies of former Odolagas which I did not fear but, being untrained, could not dispel. The cone was an uneasy place at any time, shape so out of keeping with the general pattern of ridge, valley and great highlands. On this side of the mountain more birds were flying to roost than I had noticed on the south. Two pairs of ravens flapped over to some ledge in undiscovered cliffs, and when it was black night a loud *hoo hoo* close to and on a level with my face made me lie still until I identified the caller: an eagle owl sitting under an awning of ivy on a branch lower down the steep slope, ears erect and staring at me with faintly luminous eyes so that it appeared a child-sized, fat, horned imp disapproving the intruder.

She could go on disapproving. A half-moon was up and it was time to be on the move. I started off to do the round of the plateau, crossing to the curious outcrop of rocks where the escarpment began to rise from the ridge. The nesting place of the ravens was there, and with it a surprise. The plateau ended abruptly at a sheer precipice so deep that the slanting moonlight could not show me the bottom. I could hear water surging down the gorge. Its far side, worn down by freshets from the mountain, was not so sheer but quite unclimbable.

After following the edge until I was satisfied that this torrent must discharge, not far below the amphitheater, into the stream I knew, I walked along the north side of the plateau to see if I could spot any particular track which Odolaga would take when he rode up through the woods from his house. All the way the main flock of sheep were on my left, lying down and undisturbed by my gentle pace. Several times I glimpsed a shadow moving parallel to me and wondered if there were still wolves in the fastnesses of the Pyrenees. It seemed unlikely, for in that case there should be dogs on guard and perhaps a shepherd as well. But the shadow did turn out to be a shepherd: the black goat was on duty, keeping always between me and the flock. He would not come near me, and if I had turned towards the sheep he would, I think, have had them quickly on their feet and bunched.

Then I returned to my base and slept until again I could see the plateau and a short pyramid of cone above the mist.

## August 23

It was the eagle owl who first put a possible plan into my head. That my objective must be the goat I had decided when I first saw it, but the mere slaughter of the beast was insufficient. Whatever devilry Odolaga had performed on Rita would not be reversed because an unknown brute had killed his familiar and vanished; and when he realized — as I meant him to — that I, come all the way from Penminster, was the assassin, he was more likely to intensify his attack than relinquish it.

So there had to be a tiger brother fraud to convince him that I was as adept a shaman as he, dangerous and not to be offended with impunity. That was where my friend, the eagle owl, came in. I call her my friend because she

135

had no fear of me. She reminded me of my half-wild Indian owl, presenting much the same silhouette, though four times the size. She glided in from her hunting and settled on her branch. It was her daytime roost. She had been the satisfied tenant of the ivy house for years, as proved by a six-inch-deep deposit of pellets on the ground, and she didn't give a damn if I chose to squat on my patch of earth higher up the slope.

Paddy and Uncle Izar were both able to entrance birds. Remembering how Leyalá had planed down from the pediment onto my shoulder and how for an ecstatic moment I had transmitted to him our unity, I was convinced that I too had — or well might have — inherited the gift of simple hypnosis, though none of the advanced technique of Odolaga. In case it turned out that I was to that extent a shaman, I started to prepare my bow and arrows.

I had intended to kill Odolaga if all else failed. Given the wild and broken country, the unknown and untraceable murderer would be away before the body was found, and when found it might take the forensic consultant some time to decide that an arrow was the cause of death. That arrow had to be manufactured on the spot; I was not going to leave a promising clue behind me by carrying arrows through Customs or buying them in Spain. My chief difficulty had been to invent an efficient and easily fitted head. While I was trying in my studio at home to design an improvement on the Birhor method of fastening head to shaft with fine sinews, it suddenly occurred to me that the answer was in my hand at that moment. A shaft driven home into the lower half of a ball-point pen, the socket for the point evenly crushed by pliers and smoothed with a file, would do very well at close range even if discharged with less than Birhor force.

I longed for a Birhor bow — with which I could hit  a

136

matchbox at forty feet, rather better than my head-quarters officers could perform with a revolver. As it was, I had to make do with a crude longbow. Leaving my owl to sleep off her midnight snacks, I wandered through that thick, temperate forest searching for a branch or sapling that would serve. No difficulty with the arrows. I came across a species of mountain ash with stiff, straight twigs which only needed smoothing. Tradition has it that the rowan repels witches, but this one must have recognized me as a harmless amateur and allowed its shoots to be stroked and stripped. The bow gave me trouble, for I could not know the properties of the available woods. The ultimate choice was between hazel, an ash sapling or a stout shoot of beech growing straight up towards the light.

I chose the beech and spent the rest of the day working on my weapons. For the primitive hunter that task takes far more time than the hunt itself. The arrows were easy enough to trim, fletch, bind and notch. The beech bow had to be whittled down to an even thickness and the ends slightly tapered. I dared not shape it correctly for fear of weakening it. When strung it was the devil to pull and I doubted if it would have enough spring after any prolonged shooting. However, I only needed some practice shots and then one or at the most two for business; those, I could guarantee, would send the arrow slap through Odolaga or his black, comely shepherd, with the point sticking out the other side.

Tiger brother did not like owls. He treated them with respect rather than fear and had many stories about them. An owl could drive away an ancestral and benevolent spirit just when it was needed; an angry or vengeful ghost could wail like an owl or use the owl to wail for it. I was never sure which. That was one of the many cases when mind was indistinguishable from matter and language was unclear about the difference.

At any rate this fascinating creature of the night with its eerie call has been considered a bird of ill omen from time immemorial. It turns up in the environment of witches, though rarely as a familiar. I suspect that the shamans of the English kept live or dead owls like skulls and stuffed reptiles to impress the customers rather than for any real use, but to Uncle Izar the long tradition of the owl could have more meaning than to me. Divination, if there is such a thing? To help in creating illusion for enemy or patient? So it seemed likely that the appearance of an owl at the scene of a disaster would be more significant to him than any other bird, and that since my whole object was to cloak a tiger brother fraud in mystery and entice the shaman into worrying that he might be up against a rival with all his own powers and more, the owl was a valuable stage property.

Before making use of my large and alarming friend, I had to know whether I could reach the far side of the gorge and escape from it unseen. So when at last the bow was ready and tested and there were still three hours before sunset, I again hid my pack and weapons and set off through the woods on my side of the plateau. I soon came to a rough path running along the lip of the gorge. The edge was not so clean as on the grassland, tree roots having split and tumbled the rocks, but there was no possible way down until I came to a clearing where the path dived into a cleft by way of ledges and steps cut through the worst of the rubble. Crossing the fast, shallow stream at the bottom, I found a zigzag path up the other side. Along the top was little cover except rocks, but I thought they would serve at night. The most satisfying discovery was that the path allowed me to cross the gorge in a

138

matter of minutes. I could get away around the base of the peak, a route which I already knew, or along the far side of the gorge and downhill to the confluence of the streams. Whichever Odolaga chose, I could take the other.

I was back in time to watch him make his evening visit. He came up as the day before over the far edge of the plateau and into sight. The sheep were on my side, near the boundary of the trees. When the black goat got up to greet him, it was closely followed by the leader of the flock, a fine ewe, black-faced like many of the others but distinguishable by a white crescent or horseshoe above the nose. The rest followed her, so that the scene was comically like a parade. The colonel and his adjutant faced the company commander and the troops behind her standing at ease in mild curiosity as to what would happen next. Nothing did. Odolaga played with and petted his familiar and then rode off. Company commander and the rest wandered off and lay down or browsed near the skyline above the gorge.

As the sun dipped behind the mountain, its long and gloomy shadow turned the sheep from white to gray. It was time to experiment with the eagle owl. I was sure that I could make her sit still and possibly fly to me — unless she chose to attack — but I wanted more than that: to hypnotize her as Odolaga, according to Concha Pirrone, had hypnotized Leyalá. Of his more complex technique which had nearly destroyed me I knew nothing.

I held the owl's eyes as she stared at me and either received or guessed something of her simple, passing thoughts. I was harmless. I was food (not to eat but to start up by my movements). I had eyes owlish rather than animal. Strangely, I was in danger myself of being hypnotized; that is to say, there was some degree of mutual trance. Tiger brother when curing a mentally disturbed patient called it a drawing out of the soul. The trance became ecstatic, the preliminary to the mystic vision, and I could only preserve my own individuality within the communion by an effort of will, forcing the life that was me to remember its very mundane object. Trance must have been reinforced, for I found that I had succeeded. The owl loosened her grip on the branch and fell softly onto the carpet of pellets. I tied feet and bill and propped her up against the tree.

Blue dusk had now vanished. It was a still night and the highlands sang with silence broken only by the calling of other owls and a short spell of distant barking from the dogs at Odolaga's manor. I fitted my pack on my shoulders and crept out along the wooded edge of the plateau as far as the gorge, then turned left along it, crouching low to be out of sight of the sheep. At intervals I crawled up the slope and lay still, trying to make out the shape of the black goat. I could not spot him until I had the light of both half-moon and brilliant Jupiter, giving a visibility of over a hundred yards. Well away from the flock, he was standing on duty above the path by which his master or any other creature would arrive. It's probable that there was seldom any movement up from the trackless forest on the other side where I had established my lair.

He stood head on to me for a time, curious but not suspicious. My motionless outline with the pack on my back was that of a lump or a cluster of flowers. The position in which I wanted him was half-turned-away, so that I could aim the arrow behind the shoulder and through the heart. I dared not risk calling him to me. We had to remain strangers condemned to be enemies. If he had come in the hope of finding a human with whom to pass an affectionate moment, I should never have been able to betray his trust and butcher him.

140

He started to graze a little. When he was in position I rose slowly to my knees and the next instant he was dead. The arrow is so much more in keeping with nature and our inevitable death than steel or the bullet. It strikes like the hawk, out of silence and back to silence.

I withdrew the arrow, broke it and thrust the pieces into the ground. Then I dragged him by the horns to the precipice and threw him over. The sheep had not stampeded, for I was on lower ground and only my head was visible, if that. When I returned from the edge they were bunched behind the dominant ewe, who was looking in my direction but could not see me and was not yet ready to bolt. She may have been waiting for a lead from the black shepherd, always alert to whatever was going on.

It was then that the idea of completing both mystery and retribution came to me. My plan so far had not been oversuccessful, for when Odolaga searched for his familiar and found him at the bottom of the gorge it would not take him long to discover the very material wound. But if the black goat were partly squashed by a rock or other falling objects the cause of death would remain obscure, and the lunacy which had taken the goat over the precipice could be ascribed to possession or whatever evil influence Odolaga preferred.

I circled around the leading ewe out of her sight, and when she was directly between me and the gorge I imitated as best I could a terrified bleating; it was really the bleating of a fawn caught by man or a predator, but I hoped that in essence it was the same as that of a lamb. The ewe boldly made a few steps towards the sound and was met by the coughing snarl of an angry tiger — which, since I am of its clan, I can produce perfectly. She knew nothing of tigers but every gene in her body recognized that such a sound meant death. In blind sheep-panic she galloped, as I foresaw she would, straight away from me followed by the flock. They hurtled down the steepening slope and over the precipice, the protracted thuds at the bottom growing softer as there were more bodies to fall on. Depth and distance prevented the immolation being heard by human ears at Odolaga's house beyond the home woods, but his dogs heard and their frantic, warning barks broke out into the silence.

Now for my eagle owl. When I returned to her, she was beating the air, glaring with fury and quite helpless. After smoothing the great furry wings to her side and lashing them with the bowstring, I tucked her under my arm and was relieved to find how light she was in spite of her size, certainly not more than ten pounds. Then we took the forest path to the crossing of the gorge and up the other side, where the scattered boulders were smaller than I thought and gave inadequate cover. At last I chose a black outcrop of rock right at the brink behind which I could safely kneel. I should be able to get away unseen while Odolaga was running off towards one or other of the two points of access to the gorge.

During the period of waiting for him to arrive I began to hate myself. In spite of the depth of the precipice, there was a continuous murmur of muffled strugglings. The death of his familiar I had planned; the mass murder of the flock was an unexpected bonus offered and immediately accepted. It should not have been accepted. I had put myself on a level with Odolaga. Though my magic was a fraud from beginning to end, it was black magic of the worst. The horrified jury in the Wincanton court would rightly have judged me guilty. What would Paddy have said? Perhaps that I had abused religion. And tiger brother? He, having approved the triumph of the clan,

142

would still be doubtful whether the ancestral spirits agreed and would perform the rites necessary to convince them. A long way around to satisfy an uneasy conscience.

However, there was no going back. I had been so appallingly successful that it occurred to me that after all Odolaga might not accept that I, known to have inherited a shaman's fellowship with other animals but nothing more, could be responsible. He too might search conscience after such an inexplicable disaster and never see that it was a warning from me to keep away from the scene of Paddy's murder and to set Rita free from her lethargy of spirit. He might believe it to be the revenge of some other enemy; or it might be the dark cone itself, which seemed capable of any malignancy if the Presence did not receive whatever sacrifices he made to it. A wild and primitive conjecture! But nothing would have induced me to live under the shadow of that uncanny mountain.

It was hardly wise to sign my name, but I did the next best. I broke the bow into two halves, throwing one away and driving the other into the ground. In a deep slit at the top I left a note:

WITH THE COMPLIMENTS OF LEYALÁ

He came into sight across the gorge, striding out firmly with two dogs at his heels. He stopped, looking all around for his black goat, and then noticed how scattered were the very few survivors of the flock. Assuming that the rest had for some reason gone down into the woods, he sent his dogs racing off to find them. He came nearer to the precipice, heard a faint baaing from some dying sheep and shone a flashlight on the scene below.

143

I slipped the lashings from the owl's talons, then from the wings, while I held her between my legs, and lastly from the beak, heaving her into the air too fast for her to punish me. For a moment she settled on the rock to recover lucidity and balance and then took off, a ghostly creature with a five-foot wingspread, yet without a sound in the air from the soft feathers. Her *hoo hoo*, twice repeated, sounded like laughter as twice she circled over Odolaga.

He fell on his knees in the attitude of prayer. When he stood up, the tears streaming down his face sparkled like the drip of icicles in the light of the moon. He did not rush off with the dogs to find cause or culprit as I expected he would. He turned back slowly towards his house to recover himself and, I suppose, to get help, to rouse men, to drive tractor and trailer up into the gorge from the meeting of the waters.

So my escape was anticlimax. I walked off as he had done — but somewhat faster — and scrambled down into the bed of the stream, following its course for mile after mile so that no dogs could track me, till I was clear of the gorge, and at first light passed through those flowered and idyllic valley meadows which I had taken so much trouble to avoid on my outward journey. I was utterly exhausted and careless, but the hill farmers and their children slept late and I think I was never seen. Later I remembered that it was Sunday. At last I hit the path on which I had started out three days before, and when I came to a tangled grove on the hillside where a deer or a wet and staggering man could lie up in safety, I entered it and rested and at last slept.

In the morning it was raining, of which I was glad since I should appear at the bus stop evenly wet all over rather than from mid-thigh down. I flapped along, now more careful to avoid the scattered homesteads, and chose a moment when no one was in sight to cross the Bayonne road and vanish into the valley on the other side. Then I made a difficult circuit so that when I approached the village lower down the pass I should be seen descending from the hills to the east. Nowhere have I left any trace of my presence beyond the private warning to Odolaga.

My luck was in. There was a bus from the frontier due in about an hour and a blessed village tavern where I was warmed and restored by good red wine and a pan of eggs with high-powered red sausages. I still had some of my Pamplona salami left. It will be long before I want to taste it again, but I must admit that as spicy and easily portable nourishment for the fugitive it is hard to beat.

While I waited, vast, black clouds gathered so swiftly that I could not tell whether they had come from the hot plains of France or Spain. The Pyrenees roared with the echoing anger of mountain thunder. The genial, French-speaking old lady who had served me stood at the window watching the fireworks. Twice the lightning struck on the tip of a cone just visible to the northwest which I knew only too well. I noticed that she crossed herself, which she had not done even for a strike just across the road.

"*Aquelarre*," she murmured.

I thought that was probably Basque for "God save us" or something of the sort, but it turned out to be the local name of the mountain.

"It's what we call it around here," she said, " — the Hill of the He-goat. Lightning always strikes it. Old people say it is because the Devil lives there. What superstition! No doubt it is made of iron."

"But you did cross yourself, madame," I reminded her.

145

"That is because my grandmother told me to. And the foolishness one does as a child one continues without thinking."

I have no comment except that the slopes of Aquelarre showed no sign of iron ore.

The bus took me down to Pamplona, where I changed into dry clothes in the garage where I had left my car. And so I drove away to Huesca, as I had come, and over the frontier to Toulouse, where I am staying for a couple of nights relishing modernity and writing up this journal, not omitting the victory and the human guilt as in any other war diary.

# VIII

## August 27

I do not know what to make of myself. Nothing new
about that. Conscience is uneasy, still accusing me of bru-
tality, but conscience can go to hell. Rita, my Rita, is
herself again and more adorable than ever. So Uncle Izar
has come to respect the power of his rival shaman —
black comedy if only I could make sense of the process
by which he returned her soul at a distance. I must accept
that there is far more in this tradition called magic than
bullocks and birds and familiars and telepathy, and that I
have only touched the fringe of many ways to exploit the
unity of life for good or for evil.

With it all I am a very different man from the poor creature who drove away from Penminster. I have added action to knowledge, am complete and feel it. My only anxiety is the escape of Meg — but the bond between us is too close for her to have gone far.

My first thought on returning home this afternoon was Rita. I did not have to wait for news of her. She was in the house with Ginny, taking advantage of my absence to shake and dust all cleanable objects and rearrange them with such ingenuity that nothing is where it should be. At least they had some regard for the studio and left it alone.

I was shaken when Rita threw her arms around me and kissed me. Apparently she had told Ginny that I was likely to arrive that day — a premonition worthy of tiger brother since they had had no word from me. "Ginny always wanted to have a go," she said, "but she wouldn't until I gave her moral support." I should not have thought Ginny needed it; but it is true that I have left everything much as it was in my father's day and lately got into the habit of telling her not to bother with this and that.

Rita pointed out that it was due to living in the forest. "Instead of moving the litter away from the hut you got used to moving the hut away from the litter."

Not wholly true. It was the camp we moved, not the hut. A stab of memory brought up the state of her cottage when I last saw it.

"I know what you are thinking," she said. "Darling Alfgif, forget it! I don't know what came over me, but it has gone."

I asked her when she began to feel better.

"Soon after you lent me Ginny, and a day or two later the sun came out."

That must have been when I was on the prowl towards Odolaga but before I got to work on him.

"And you — you're looking so brown and young and well. What did you do in Paris? Lunch out of doors every day?"

"Yes, and up half the night."

"And here was I thinking you were all stuck into mysticism with your Indian friend. Any good garden restaurants where you would like to take me?"

Any and every, my Rita, with petals drifting on the wind into your hair. But I answered: "Only a rather gloomy place called Aquelarre."

Under cover of the busy vacuum cleaner I left them and drove off to collect Meg from George Midwinter. He told me that she had escaped the night before and overwhelmed me with apologies. "I couldn't foresee it . . . it seemed impossible . . . just come and look!"

He led me to the special home he had prepared for Meg — not a proletarian cage as for the various convalescents but a closed shed, its only door opening into the house, with a wooden floor, plenty of straw for burrowing, a new blanket and even a toy. Meg had eaten her way out, starting from a crack in the floorboards which she had enlarged to an irregular hole just wide enough to squeeze through. She had then burrowed through the earth under the shed. Splinters were scattered around, some with black hairs sticking to them, and a little powdery soil flung out from the tunnel.

George told me that he had had a few dogs staying the night after minor operations and thought at first that their whimpering and barking might have upset Meg.

"But it was the other way around. When I looked over my patients in the morning, I found signs that the most active had been trying to get out as well — floors scratched, wood chewed, and the most intelligent of them had actually left tooth marks on locks and latches. I am sure it was Meg who started the rout. You weren't calling her, were you?"

I assured him that I wasn't, and that at the time I was driving through the night to the car ferry at Boulogne.

"Or she calling you?"

I replied that I was not Paddy, and while Meg and I were responsive to each other in contact or near it, I had no idea how to influence her at a distance.

"That sounds as if you thought it possible," he said.

I told him that given the community of all life I wouldn't rule it out and added, more cautiously, that when he came across something as inexplicable as his mad dog which was perfectly healthy after all, the influence of another animal, including man, was a hypothesis to be explored.

But both of us were too worried to play about with anything but the facts. George swore that he had looked for her everywhere and informed his morning clients and even the police. No one had seen Meg.

"You told Ginny?" I asked.

"Yes, at once. Ginny called and called but couldn't find her. She doesn't seem to be in the house or garden."

I said that she would be in the woods where I had painted her and again and again we had played together. I was reasonably sure of it and that she would come looping over the ground to my call. If she had been in an accident in Penminster or crossing a road we should have heard of it.

What surprised me was that Ginny had not told me at once of Meg's disappearance and evidently had not mentioned it to Rita. When I got back and found that Rita had left, I asked Ginny why she had said nothing.

"Because I wants you to see when you comes back that Miss Rita was past her little trouble and as sweet and merry as we knows her. If I'd started up on that Meg, 'twould have been Meg and Meg as soon as you'd crossed the threshold instead of her being all over you as she was, the poor dear."

Sentimental old thing! But I am glad of it. And of course she thinks nothing of calling our learned, lovely neighbor "poor dear" for some good reason of her own.

## August 29

The man has left me disturbed. I have no fear of him and my uneasiness in no way resembles the neurosis which Odolaga wished on me. I might call it awe. I feel as if I were walking on the ridge between two hidden valleys. I do not know the path and the wreathing of mist curls around me so that I can neither step off it nor go ahead with the confidence of Julian Molay.

I had always hoped that I should meet again that eccentric connoisseur of painting, Paddy's Middle Eastern customer whom he sent to me in March before his death. I knew so much less of Paddy than I do now and had then no reason to suppose that their common interests extended beyond hunting saddles.

Early this morning Molay telephoned me from Frome that he was riding south across the downs to see something of the country and could pass near me. Would I permit him to look once more at my work? I replied at once and warmly that I could supply reasonable entertainment for horse and man and hoped he would come to lunch. So I asked Ginny to do her best and I put some order into the studio.

I went out to meet him when I heard him trotting up the drive. It was still impossible to guess his age — somewhere between fifty-five and seventy — but he looked younger than the El Greco grandee whom I remembered. That may have been due to his seat and his regal partnership with the horse: an Anglo-Arab stallion which, when I greeted it, put ears forward and bowed its head to my hand with proper Eastern courtesy. It was a beauty, the epitome of graceful maleness with a touch of savagery. One could imagine it ruling the herd of mares in some illimitable grassland and challenging with complete assurance predator or rival. I asked Molay where he had managed to borrow or hire such a splendid creature, assuming that he had not brought it over all the way from the Syrian shore. He had bought it the day before, and had apparently paid lordly cash and taken delivery at once in person.

I am no horseman. In my Indian days anything, horse or mule, that would get me reliably from place to place would do. But I know enough to be sure that it was more than exceptional to take a full stallion which one had never ridden before out on a casual, cross-country tour.

"It wasn't necessary," he said. "We knew each other or our shadows."

I let that go. What he meant is a little plainer now. However, I immediately suspected that art was an excuse and that his call had something in common with von Pluwig's, though what he wanted from me was unlikely to be as simple as persuading Arminius to stop trailing his off hind or as inexplicable as holding a brick at the point of balance.

We put up the stallion in the old cattle shed, clean and with a floor of stone flags, and I brought Paddy into the conversation by saying that when he rode over occasionally to see me we did the same; he used to insist that the loose box, long unused but in fair condition, was inhospitable — an adjective hard to justify but typical of Paddy's insight.

Over lunch Molay fascinated me on the subject of the relationship between horse and man, and I thought he might be approaching the object of his visit. But then he led me on to talk about myself and my years in India, of which he already knew something from Paddy. I told him how I had spent all my leaves with a hunting tribe whose shaman had accepted me as a blood brother and how I came to respect his beliefs and many of his practices.

"What did he teach you?"

"Nothing. He didn't teach. He explained, or tried to. And I found that my conception of the unity of life was the same as his. But I haven't any of Mr. Gadsden's gifts and it's long odds against my being able to help you — if that is what you have come for."

"Ah well, there is always Meg," he said.

I apologized for Meg's absence on business, saying that I had left her at the vet's while I was abroad for some days. She had escaped but would come back.

"How can you be so sure?"

"Because I know she is alive and well."

It's hard to describe how I know; easier to describe how I would feel if she were dead. A blank. A wall. And grief rebounding from it.

"I saw her as Paddy Gadsden's familiar spirit," Molay said. "Now she is yours, I suppose."

"If you like to call our closeness that. But she meant more to Paddy than to me."

"In what way more?"

I answered that of course I had realized that Meg was a traditional familiar and that I had been curious enough to read all that the witch trials could tell me. But still I could not understand, beyond dubious theories of my own, what the use of the familiar was, and I was puzzled by the open, fearless confessions of witches that they controlled imps and willed them to do whatever was wanted.

"They must have really believed it," Molay said.

"Apparently. Another illusion like flying on a broomstick."

"Not quite the same. Drugs could create a fantasy of flying just as in what now is called a trip. No, not illusion, Mr. Hollaston, but a way of seeing — of seeing the object in terms of the object and the object in terms of its relation to you."

I could follow his meaning and I mentioned Meg's dancing and my impression that something accompanied her in the dance.

"Exactly. But you could not see that something."

"In what shape?"

"Whatever shape suited your desires. Imp or angel or that other Meg which throws no shadow."

"Then it is illusion."

"The shape you choose is illusion. The Presence is not. Take the divine Athene, the personification of a new society of justice, wisdom, beauty and civic pride! Did she exist? The question is absurd. She existed in that form because in that form she was needed."

I accept, and always have, his example of the truth behind the myth. To see what he would say, I told him that while I was recently abroad I had camped for the night on a wild and sullen hill and felt its Presence strongly but had given it no form.

"Were you afraid to give it form?"

"Neither wished nor feared. In what form should it have appeared to me?"

"Whatever you liked. Without you it has no form."

"But does exist?"

"Since it is subject to the law of cause and effect it must in some sense exist. Mr. Hollaston, Meg seems to be leading us away from the point. Would you show me again the picture you named the *Holy Well?*"

I carried the brandy into the studio and asked Ginny to serve us coffee there. She looked at my guest without her usual geniality, playing the stern housekeeper. I take it she had — forgivably — been listening at the door. She would not have made much of the conversation beyond resenting it as bearing upon an aspect of me which she distrusted. Myself I still could not guess what Julian Molay expected from his visit. When he was speaking he had a trick of turning his head slightly away, keeping his eyes on me. His hawk nose and the keen, oblique glance reminded me of the brass eagle on the lectern of a parish church, though in his case the wings of revelation were folded.

When I set up the *Holy Well* he was silent for a while, seeming to look through it, not at it. That in a way was how I had meant it to be judged.

"I see now why it is so precious to you. The Presence is there but without form," he said. "Have you been so inspired before or since?"

"Perhaps in the jungle, and perhaps in this portrait of Meg."

I took down the *Holy Well* and set up *Meg.* I did not expect that he would see more than the environment to which she belonged.

"You have painted the *Meg* without a shadow" was his comment.

"She was not well. I painted it as if entranced — a direct importuning of her Purpose to heal her."

"As of course it did. Mr. Hollaston, I have never realized that the concentration of the master craftsman was a prayer."

"Nor did I till then."

"What was the matter with Meg?"

"A sending, if you know what that is. From Meg it took away her joy. To others it caused terror and madness and death."

"I take it that the terror was your own. How did you cure that?"

At last I guessed the object of his visit. It was to find out my source of power, if any, and to confront me. My Pyrenean magic had indeed been taken seriously by Odolaga, who perhaps had appealed in despair to this magnificent curiosity of a man. Undoubtedly he knew something of what had been going on. But I was angry with his pretentious transcendentalism and nearly told him to mind his own business. As it was, I set up my *Columns of the Sun*, saying that it would be hard for him to understand it.

"So that was your prayer and again it was invincible," he acknowledged, ignoring my discourtesy. "Didn't you know that you had won?"

"Afterwards, yes."

"Then why more?"

I did not see what he meant by "more." He then left me in no doubt.

"Cruelty. Slaughter without mercy. How could you abuse the divinity of man by revenge on so many happy innocents?"

"Not revenge. A warning."

"If you discovered so much, why did you not kill Leyalá?"

"Because he trusted me, damn you!"

"I cannot understand you, Mr. Hollaston. So much love and so much evil!"

I told him to go back to his friend Odolaga and remind

156

him that I could protect my loved ones as well as myself. He asked for no explanation, leaping straight to the point by, I think, no more than quick human sympathy.

"Was someone you love also affected by Leyalá?"

"No! No one could be less vulnerable."

"Then isn't what you believed impossible?"

I answered that I didn't know any longer what was possible and by what other means Odolaga could attack.

"One more question, if you will forgive a guest. When you had painted the *Columns of the Sun* and the unity was over and the spirit had returned to the dust, did you not feel empty, without faith in anything but . . ."

"My lunch, yes."

"But let us suppose that she loves you as you love her! If that were so, your black night of the soul would have affected her. Invulnerable to the sending, yes. But not to the shaman in you."

I have never wanted to suspect even the possibility and told him so, adding that if a mood of mine could affect her, hers should affect me.

"Not necessarily," he replied. "Your mind was closed. To use a term of simpler energy, you put her back on the air. Why are you celibate, Mr. Hollaston?"

"How do you know I am?"

"Because your power is so great though you know so little."

He got up and thanked me for my hospitality as if there had been no tension between us. We walked out to the cattle shed talking of pleasant routes to the west and of Paddy. There was no sign that Molay knew anything of the puzzling circumstances of Paddy's death and I did not mention them. When he had saddled and led out his stallion, I asked him if he were shipping his new beauty to Alexandretta.

"No. Only to France, where I have another home," he said.

He raised his cap and was off, leaving me numbed and uneasy, as if I were one of my innocent — but only partly innocent — ancestors waiting in the dock for the verdict of the jury.

I am out of my depth. My understanding of the hunting shaman is helpful but has become inadequate, just as observation of the ape is helpful to the sociologist but inadequate. The lines of descent, which have become extinct or hybridized into superstition, crackpot faiths and fortune-telling, have been reduced to one; and the one appears to have advanced down the millennia far beyond the cults of tiger brothers.

It may be that Paddy's motive in sending Molay to me was not only to introduce a buyer to a friend but to propose me as a future Robin. The job — what a word! — is unacceptable if still open. In the glimpses I have had, admittedly affected by Odolaga, there is too much black and none of the ecstasy. Yet I remember so vividly Odolaga playing with his shepherd-goat on that flowered alp in the stillness of the evening. Before my coming great joy was there.

## August 31

Meg is back, and it is left to me to make what I can of her return. I never dreamed that Julian Molay was responsible for her disappearance. It's a sign that this pair of Men in Black can deprive me of Meg whenever they like and also that they are, for the moment, above taking such a tit-for-tat revenge. I must expect it in some other form.

158

Bill Freeman came in with her this morning. His story was that a fine old fellow, beautifully mounted, had stopped and said good evening to him when he was digging up his potatoes in the front garden and asked if he knew to whom a tame polecat belonged. And there was Meg in front of him on the saddle, clinging to the pommel with her forefeet and happy as a hunt terrier. Bill exclaimed that she was my missing Meg and asked where the gentleman had found her. The answer was vague: that he had picked her up far down the green lane and had been riding along until he came to a likely person. When he saw Bill, he knew at once that he was the likely person.

Bill was cautious. He said that he thought highly of Miss Meg — on condition that she kept herself to herself.

To his amazement, the gentleman, who had never been seen around these parts before, said: "You're a healer yourself, if I'm not wrong."

"I am that," Bill answered. "But I use the gift our Lord 'as given me and I don't deal in the likes of Miss Meg."

The gentleman had replied that blessed are the pure in heart and that Meg was no different from himself.

"And then 'e rides off," Bill went on, "and when Meg sees 'im go she sits up with 'er little paws dangling like she was praying" — myself, I call that the prelude to the dance, but "praying" will do — "and she comes in and after supper climbs onto the missus' shoulder and the missus starts feedin' 'er with bits of bacon and she stays there till we goes to bed when we puts 'er in a basket before the kitchen fire."

What kindliness to a very suspect fugitive! I was glad to hear that Meg had not lost her manners. Ordinarily she hates bacon.

"What did the cats make of her?" I asked.

"Wouldn't 'ave nought to do with her nor she with them.

There's one thing I always say about cats. None of 'em ain't got no religion."

"And dogs?"

"They bows down before us sinners, Mr. Alfgif, like the 'eathen before wood and stone."

I'll pass over my meeting with Meg. She expressed our unity better than I could, diving into my pocket, where she stayed trembling with pleasure. I don't know how Molay spotted a fellow shaman — tiger brother too had no trouble — but I do see one reason why he chose Bill Freeman to return Meg. He was sure that Bill would repeat everything he said and that I should sense a gentleness which I might have missed.

I took advantage of this new intimacy with Bill Freeman to find out more about my great-great-grandfather who taught the art of exterminating warts to Bill's grandmother.

"What did she think of him?"

"Wanted to teach 'er more than that, 'e did. But she wouldn't 'ave nothing to do with it."

"Did he ever have a pet like Meg?"

" 'E was never without 'is dogs alongside 'im, Mr. Alfgif, or so they say."

"I didn't mean dogs and horses."

"Well, if you means what I thinks you means, that was why my grandmother wouldn't 'ave no more to do with 'im."

"Had it got a forked tail and all that?" I asked.

"Well, if it did, she didn't tell me. All she said was that it were a little chap no 'igher than a newborn calf. And when she tells Mr. Hollaston that she's seen in the dairy what she didn't ought to 'ave, 'e says: ' 'E ain't there not in a manner of speaking, but you can see 'im anytime you wants to. And you know I wouldn't do nothing wrong,

160

Betsy.' 'That you wouldn't,' she tells 'im, 'for a kinder gentleman there never was, sir. But little people aren't for the likes of me whether they ain't really there or not,' she says. 'Well then, Betsy my love,' 'e says, 'I 'ad 'opes of you but we'll say no more about it. And don't you forget what I learned you and you pass it on!' "

"So he never said what it was?"

"Now blowed if you 'aven't put summat into my mind, Mr. Alfgif, because 'e did tell 'er what it wasn't. 'It ain't a child nor a calf,' 'e says, 'and it ain't a stream or a tree or a flower,' 'e says. 'It's the whole blessed valley and because we loves it, it loves us, and you wouldn't like to be in love and not be seen nohow,' 'e says."

Bill Freeman, with his earnest Christian faith and that small pagan practice which faintly disturbs the vicar, is indeed pure in heart, as Molay perceived. I remember asking him what would happen if he tried to kill anything larger than a wart by thinking, and he replied that it would be straight evil. So it would be. Yet I have allowed those two Men in Black to believe that was just the sin I committed. My education never stops. Here is great-great-grandfather repeating to me down a century and a half exactly what Molay said: that where there is a Presence you can see it in any shape you like.

I wonder if Molay's theory of the cause of Rita's lethargy could possibly be right. Looking back through the pages of this notebook I see that after I had painted *Columns of the Sun* and destroyed Odolaga's sending, I did fall into a black night without faith in any purpose or Purpose. This meant that all my receptors were out of action. However, the shaman's transmitter — I am compelled by now to grant myself some such power — could still be effective. And what was it transmitting? Apathy, nihilism, self-contempt and resentment that my ancient home should be turned into a playground for obsolete religion. Very well! But nobody should have been one penny the worse.

Yet suppose that Rita's receptors were wide open to me as Molay suggested. Leave love out of it, which I dare not believe. Our intimate friendship, her interest and help in the terror that haunted me, her discovery of the probable reason for Odolaga's assault — all those created so close a bond that my moods and thoughts could affect her. That is common enough in a close marriage. The unspoken depression of one affects the other and neither realizes it.

It was natural enough that I should put the blame on Odolaga, though I could never understand quite how his quick visit to the Pirrones gave the opportunity nor how he could be certain, merely from Concha's chatter of a pastoral flirtation, that Rita was more precious to me than myself. And indeed I was too angry and impatient to accept that Rita is as safe from curses as any missionary or politician. The deliberate attack of a witch doctor would not be received by her at all.

Then how about her recovery during my absence? Well, even that falls into place. It had nothing to do with a poor, slaughtered goat and owls and night and Aquelarre. It was due to my own recovery, pride, cunning and cruelty filling up the void of my mind together with a primitive relish in carrying a tiger brother deception — which he himself would have condemned — from India to the Pyrenees.


## September 2

That call which Meg answered, burrowing her way to freedom, was a general summons. George's patients all received it and tried to get out, but only Meg could. It must have been transmitted directly at fairly close quarters and is no different in kind from my experiment with bullocks. I have had my punishment or a part of it. Molay has evened the score, but if he hoped to destroy all communion between me and my familiar he has failed.

He hardly entered my thoughts during this afternoon which began so happily. Rita and I were pushing our way between branches on the far side of the valley. She claimed to have found some evidence that on the rising ground above the water, now so densely covered by trees, there was once a Saxon settlement. Since I knew every foot of the woodland I was sure there was no sign of trench or mound, but jumped at the chance to be together. I did not take Meg, for Rita faintly resents her. I wouldn't call it jealousy — more annoyance because Meg distracts my attention.

We discovered no trace of our ancestors — I expect they had lived at Penminster and merely cleared the land — so we sat on the first slope of the downs with the bright green of the cattle paradise at our feet and beyond it the whole length of the valley in its hard, full maturity with darkening leaves clustered over seed. The oaks of the parkland drooped above the close-cropped turf, each far enough from its neighbor to preserve individuality, yet each, like ourselves, drawing peace and security from the fellowship.

"They draw security from you," she said when I had mentioned something of the sort.

"Or I from them. Unless it is a sapling which I myself have planted, I never feel that I own a tree. It owns me."

"You could only feel that here, not in your Indian jungle."

She was right. There the feeling is quite different. Individuality is swamped. Everything, animal and vegetable, is one, demanding space but dependent on the unity.

"Could you respond to a fern as you do to Meg?" she asked, smiling at me.

"Not unless I see the fern without a shadow as well as the fern."

"And which am I? The Rita without a shadow or Rita?"

I said that she was always both.

"But suppose Rita was tired of staying behind the *Holy Well*?"

I laughed that off, unwilling to give it meaning, and said that I would let her out by painting her mirror image on the back of the canvas.

One complex of regrets having been forcibly suppressed, another had the time to take over. The sheep under the oaks, now massed, now scattered, reminded me of Odolaga's flock — his in the peace of the great upland grazing on grasses rougher than mine and rippled by wind, these in a rich, manmade English peace. But as I looked down the stream to the wooded hillside where my vixen had lived and horribly died, conscience relaxed. Whether I was right or wrong in holding Odolaga responsible for Rita's melancholy, he had deserved what I sent him.

When we were back at my house with drinks in front of us, I abandoned Rita for a moment to fetch Meg in case she wished to join us. I had left her curled up in the studio and asleep. I found that she had been busy in my absence and had made herself a nest. That was a trick of hers when occasionally she was bored with arranging shavings or straw and wanted to try her hand at domesticity. I assumed that she had torn the stuffing out of an armchair and rearranged it on the floor, but closer inspection showed that the fragments were of canvas. She had ripped the *Holy Well* from its stretcher and nibbled it to pieces. Together with *Columns of the Sun* it had been leaning against the wall where I had put them after Molay's visit. *Columns* had been spared with only a hole in the corner.

I could not look at that debris. I turned away. Meg started to climb up my leg. I put her down. I hope my hand was gentle. I think it was. Only then did it flash into my mind that she could be as innocent as Leyalá. A fine, new example of the familiar trained into a curse! And it was Molay who was responsible, not Odolaga mourning far away in his own valley. He had had Meg in his possession long enough to imprint on her what she had to do.

The *Holy Well* is gone forever. It was the only work of mine which all the world could understand. Any stroller through a gallery would have stopped in front of it and wondered how it was that he could feel an unseen, unknown behind the water. Of no other painting can I be so sure. *Columns of the Sun* is private and intelligible only to the mystic. *Meg* is only a woodland scene until the eye picks up that the composition is that of a portrait. Never again perhaps can I bring together this world and the world without a shadow. My Presence is not visible like that of great-great-grandfather, but at least I was able to show it as more than an illusion.

When I came down again to Rita, with Meg still sleepy in my pocket, she asked me what the matter was and I told her. Among all her expressions of sorrow and sympathy there is one which I treasure. She cried: "Oh, poor Meg!"

I saw what she meant: that Meg could suffer from the loss of my love as much as I from the destruction of the *Holy Well*. Typical of my quick, generous Rita! For her as for me love is a force of the Purpose as plainly as gravity, and nothing is less endurable than a brutal end to it.

I assured her that it was not Meg's fault and that I understood what had affected her. Meg confirmed it by climbing to my shoulder and nibbling my ear. It was impossible to go into the details.

When I had driven her home she wanted me to stay, still offering comfort and devotion and not wishing me to be alone. I would not stay. Some futile excuse or other.

I called up George. It beat me how Molay could have known that Meg had been left with him, and I asked if anyone had made inquiries about her during my absence.

"Yes. Several of your friends wanted to know how she was. I suppose they thought she would be pining for you. All Penminster knows her, Alf. And when the butcher came in for a kitten to be spayed, he brought along a fine, fresh, bloody sheep kidney as a present for her."

Well, there it was. Molay had only to send someone into Penminster — perhaps a groom, perhaps a disciple — who could lead the chat in the bar of the Royal George to the subject of unusual pets or the breeding of polecat ferrets and he would hear of Meg and learn that if he wanted to see her, Mr. Hollaston was away and she was an honored guest at the vet's. I think Molay would have known without being told that she was not in a cage but running free.


## September 4

I am weary of all this pain and nonsense brought on me because Paddy chose to be discreetly killed by my car and because I could have discovered the murderer. Yet I cannot reject my inherited receptors and the teachings of the forest and so recover the enviable sanity of, let's say, some determined European accountant utterly impervious to

166

the witch doctor employed, as a last resort, by the minister of state whose books need auditing.

Yesterday evening I could not find my satchel, which I always leave on the floor inside the front door. It contains the simpler tools of my trade — pencils, crayons and a large sketch pad — so that I can grab it at a moment's notice if any object in the outside world has caught interest and imagination. I had not missed it, since the last few days have been too full of regrets and inner turmoil for me to consider the sudden vision of a branch, a cloud or a reflection as worth an attempt to record its singularity. So I went over to Ginny's apartment to ask her if she remembered where she and Rita had managed to put it. In the studio, she said. How right! That is where I never need it but where for tidy femininity it should be.

Ginny played the hostess and as it was teatime plied me with her scones, for which I have been greedy since a boy. Meg, beyond a lick of butter, did not approve but was eager for crumbled dog biscuits. I have long suspected that Ginny had a secret, special treat for her but have never guessed what it was.

She hoped that the picture which Meg had eaten — thank God Meg hadn't or a poisoned polecat would have been added to retribution! — was not valuable. She supposed it wasn't, as I had not sold it. She had seen me showing my work to that high-and-mighty gentleman when she brought coffee into the studio.

"But Miss Rita was in a rare taking about it," she told me.

I asked her how she knew. She said that she didn't ought to tell me but it would do me a power of good. On the evening of the disaster, after I had driven Rita home and left, Rita had walked up the valley in the dusk and knocked on Ginny's door. She had explained to Ginny what had happened and begged her to keep an eye on me.

"I thought as how your old trouble might be coming back, Mr. Alfgif, but she said no it weren't that, but you might run off into the woods all night or you might be getting at the whisky and tearing up your pictures all by yourself."

Ginny had not been able to understand what all the fuss was about. After all, if Meg had chewed up a picture I could always paint another. She told Rita that I was doing nothing out of the ordinary but hadn't eaten anything. Rita insisted that they should sneak around the house and look through the window at me; so they did. The whisky, as expected, was at my side, but I appeared to be lost in thought with Meg on my knee. That was quite true. I was silently cursing my art, my impotence and Molay, but I was a long way from blowing my brains out, if that was what Rita feared. Anyway, I had thrown all my cartridges into the stream when I used to be half tempted to kill myself at the time of the haunting. After that I could only think of swallowing varnish, which Gargary could probably deal with, or falling on my hunting knife like a despairing Roman, which I was sure to bungle, or electrocuting myself from the wrong side of the fuse box, which might burn down the house.

In fact it must be very rare for any master craftsman, as Molay called me, to kill himself unless drugged or drunk. Every work is succeeded by another and he clings to life in order to finish it, right up to the last, which he has to leave undone.

"I don't know why you think she ain't good enough for you, Mr. Alfgif," Ginny went on.

I replied that she was too good for me and that Oxford professors, which she would certainly become, did not

168

need a husband hanging around. (In fact I should guess that is just what they do need, pace Women's Lib.)

"Besides, what makes you think I'm in love with her?" I added.

Her answer to that was a snort. But from my behavior it cannot be obvious.

It looks as if Molay might be right and that it was I, not Odolaga, who reduced her to a state halfway between exasperation and lassitude. Poor darling, then she must be as miserably unfulfilled as I. What damned Victorian sentimentalist wasted good paint on some half-draped female leaning against a door and called the crap *Love Locked Out*? But for her sake the door must stay shut. She returns to her college in a few days. If she comes back at Christmas I must arrange to be away.

After I left Ginny I walked down through the parkland to search for comfort under the oaks. Unity . . . unity . . . but the only unity I want is denied me.

I was glad to fall in with Victor Pirrone enjoying a stroll through the late evening. Any human being would have served to compel my thoughts out of the all-embracing sense of failure and into politeness. But Victor I like more and more and am at ease with him. He has fallen completely under the enchantment of our valley and can often be found there on weekends walking up the stream. He would, I am sure, prefer to have his Concha with him, but those dainty feet break all the laws of mammalian support.

As we went on together he said surprisingly that he was glad he did not know the valley when he bought the Manor House or he would have made me an offer for it.

"But why glad?" I asked.

"Too great a responsibility. At home we would say that it has two owners — you, my dear Alf, and another. So often superstition expresses a genuine reverence. How right the ancients were to give a spring its nymph and a wood its dryad!"

"And is that still believed in Sicily?"

"In my own valley I would not like to say it is disbelieved. But the Church has taken the innocence out of it. Once when I was a child I was certain I did see something — so clearly that I asked my mother if I should confess it as a sin. She replied very sensibly that I should not eat so many figs before going to bed."

I can see why Concha's godfather was so in favor of the marriage. Though her shipbuilding father may have said that the Pirrones and the Odolagas had nothing in common except that they had no bathrooms and kept sheep, both families recognized alongside their Catholicism a religion that was more ancient. Uncle Izar could never have thought that the young Concha herself had any receptors and he was powerless to mature her into anything more than the charming, faithful, shallow woman that she is. The next-best thing was to find her a husband whose ability would take her far in life while not wholly rejecting the influences of Aquelarre. I don't mean anything so crude as the fortune-teller's sell-equities-buy-copper sort of advice, but an occasional and wise manipulation of the future.

The resemblance between Victor and my father which I thought I had spotted turns out to be wrong. My father closed his eyes to what he did not want to believe. Victor takes manifestations of mind as a matter of course — an ironical matter of course.

"And your nymph never turned up again among the olives?" I asked.

"It wasn't a nymph. It wore a frock coat."

"Predicting your future business success."

"Predicting, Alf, that I should always be sensitive to illusion. The existence of the inexplicable doesn't worry me at all. I accept all marvels. I was born among them. Take the well-attested stigmata for example! If a monk spends his holy life meditating on the crucifixion, the appearance of the stigmata is no miracle. The miracle would be if they did not appear."

I objected that he could not call physical stigmata an illusion.

"No. What we see is fact. But the visions of the monk are illusion — so far as our world is concerned. I don't deny the truer reality of another. You may have heard of my wife's godfather, Izar Odolaga. He calls it the world without shadows. And once a physicist talked to me of a very possible antimatter world. Izar's place at Aquelarre is alive, but he can handle it. I suspect he asks ghosts to dinner. They all speak Basque."

"You find it comic?"

"Not quite. But what's the alternative? If I had Izar as an enemy I'd think every rash was the beginning of leprosy. Fortunately he's a kindly fellow and more likely to turn your leprosy into a rash."

"A healer?"

"And good at it. In old days he'd have been excommunicated and lucky to get away with that. Yet if he had been a priest he would have had pilgrims limping up from France and Spain. It seems to be only a question of whether one claims to be assisted by saints or devils."

I asked which Odolaga claimed.

"Neither. He claims only to be —" Victor hesitated for the English word — "fey, I believe it is called. By the way, it was he who told me the valley had two owners."

171

"Did he ever see the other one?"

"Well, if he did, it wouldn't be what you or I would think we saw."

He must have been quoting Uncle Izar there. It reminded me how Molay had said that if you feel a Presence you can give it any shape you like. That opened up another line of inquietude. Could an enemy of Odolaga be compelled to give it a shape he didn't like at all? I doubt if the concentration of the master craftsman would be a saving prayer. I can imagine myself painting a medieval mouth of hell until I fell into it. Better, I think, to follow tiger brother's prescription and sacrifice to great-great-grandfather until I saw the spirit of my beloved valley in the elfin shape he gave it.

"So don't eat too many figs!" Victor went on. "And since we have our own Minerva in ivory and gold, we have no need to look for nymphs. *Vae!* Our Rita returns to Oxford at the end of this week and leaves us without protection. How lucky is youth in your ancient universities, tutored by goddesses instead of the dark and droning lecturers of Italy! After such an experience one could never lose a respect for scholarship, although at the time attention was inevitably distracted from medieval history."

Even Victor is inspired by her to choose his words with love. I have not heard such eloquence from him since my capture of Leyalá.

172

# IX

## September 6

It was Meg who roused me when I was half asleep in my chair, my mind wandering through the far forest with tiger brother, disembodied by his dance of worship. Meg was scrabbling at the door trying to get out. I opened it for her and followed her to the front door. When I threw it wide and let in the night, I heard what she had heard.

I could not tell whether it was played on a pipe or on the single string of hunting man. It was a reminder of all the joy we have lost and thus of infinite melancholy, yet it had the sweetness of bird song if a bird could have the voice of an animal. The symphony, to which one listens dreaming and reasoning simultaneously, must be the highest product of the human mind, yet a shepherd pipe in the stillness of night or the freshness of dawn is the music which comes nearest to communion with all creation.

Meg looped down past the still sheep under the oaks. They did not notice us, their heads turned towards the woodland which sheltered the piper or itself piped. She was moving fast and was out of sight in the darkness when she crossed the stream, but I knew that our destinations were the same; even the stems of flowers would have bent towards this song of earth if it had not been night and petals closed. By both of us the singing was received as a summons. She would have felt no fear at all, only gladness in answering. I felt both, the fear being more in the nature of reverence than the terror transmitted by Leyalá.

Often in life we answer a summons. The receptors of saint and shaman are aware of it though eyes and ears are unaffected. But this was different. I clearly heard with ears and knew that once we were under the trees I should also see. That was where fear came in. The legend of Pan and panic of course passed through my mind and was rejected as too simple, too contrived. What I was hearing was the truth behind the myth, whether expressed by man or by my valley itself.

As I entered the trees and began to plunge uphill, the descant of creature or instrument became fainter, not louder, and I guessed where it came from: a small, open glade left by a spreading beech which had fallen and been cut up for firewood. When I reached it I saw Julian Molay sitting on the stump with Meg on his shoulder. All sense of the supernatural vanished. I asked him how on earth he did it.

"Answer me how on earth you heard it and I will tell you how I did it."

"That was how you took Meg away from the vet?"

"Of course."

"And trained her to do all the damage possible!"

"A small part of all the damage possible. I expected you to kill her."

"How could I?"

"Because in your anger you are without pity. You abused love in order to take revenge."

I knew exactly what he meant. I denied fiercely that any so-called magic was concerned in the slaughter of Odolaga's black shepherd and his sheep except perhaps in the hypnosis of that stage property, the eagle owl.

"I used the skill of the hunter," I told him, "not the skill of the shaman."

"Yet from somewhere you have the gift."

Molay was standing up now, his deep eyes condemning me. He was impressive as a judge handing out a sentence, but neither ex-colonel Hollaston nor the painter of the *Holy Well* were in a mood to be impressed.

I said that I had no power at all beyond the concentration of the master craftsman: a prayer, as he had called it. I had seen what could be effected through the trance and dancing of the shaman, and by trial and error I had found out a little of the use of the familiar: of the good which I might do by communion with Meg and of the evil which was done to me and life around me by Odolaga and his training of Leyalá.

"What you feel in me is the same as you felt in Freeman, to whom you released Meg," I added. "It is a gift from my ancestors and not of my making. My grandfather had it. My great-great-grandfather had it, and we all were named Alfgif."

"I thought your name was Alfred," he said.

"Alfred means 'Wise as an Elf.' Alfgif is 'Gift of the Elf.'"

"What has that to do with it?"

"I am told the elf is my valley. See it in any shape you like! I have never wished it to appear to me. But I too was taught to sing in silence."

I must assume that I was possessed. Having no better spell, I used the incantation of tiger brother to call a spirit of the ancestors. I had closed my eyes as I rocked to and fro in the trance so that I could neither see Molay nor any result, but on and on I chanted until I felt the Presence. When I opened my eyes and stood still except for shaking, Meg had left his shoulder and had begun to dance.

"And now what shape did you give it?" I asked.

"I saw it in the shape you gave it."

"And what was that?"

"Gentle and laughing and of the earth, Alfgif."

It was the first time he had used my name. He asked me to tell him exactly what had happened on the slopes of Aquelarre. I gave him the story from the first sight of Izar Odolaga to the making of the bow and the stampede of the terrified sheep. I fear there must have been some pride in my voice besides regret.

"You said my *Columns of the Sun* was an invincible prayer," I reminded him, "and asked if I did not know it. I did not, but I found it was. So it is true that I had no more reason to fear Odolaga. His sending had failed. You must know by now what that was."

He answered that he did know, that Odolaga in his desolation had confessed all to him.

"Very well! And then the woman I love fell ill. Her soul was captured, as a shaman would say. Was it surprising that I believed it was another of Odolaga's telepathic tricks and that I set out to warn him that my powers could be as dangerous as his?"

"You were wrong to blame him."

"I know. It was you who first made me see that I myself could be responsible and now I am sure I was. All the same I think justice has been done — if one can set the beauty of my *Holy Well* against the beauty of his dear familiar."

Molay lay back on his elbows in that unspoken courtroom of the glade and gestured to me to sit on the stump. He said that at least my motive had been more generous than Odolaga's, that I had acted from love and he only from fear for himself. "So now you shall be the judge. Ask whatever questions you like!"

"Did Odolaga kill Paddy for you?"

"He did."

"So you are the Devil!"

"In the sense of anguished clergy long ago, yes, I am."

"Is there no other devil within the Purpose?"

"I doubt it. But if evil were personified, it would be the antithesis of love. Have you forgotten the cough of the tiger which maddened sixty sheep? Man does not need a devil. He does well enough by himself."

I said that I found it hard to imagine him as that ancestral Horned God when we were talking face to face and sharing the same faith.

"I dress my mind and not my body in the innocence of the horns and tail. I do not believe that my blood or my semen will fertilize a field, but it may be that I myself can still fertilize mankind. If I cannot, if my powers fail through age, then before I infect my people with my weakness it is right to kill me and choose a successor. He is already chosen but he is still too young for the fullness of wisdom. Nothing mysterious there, my Alfgif! Even in

177

politics a party may decide on its future leader before he is quite fit to lead. Therefore I must live longer and one of us has to die in my place. Paddy chose to do so. I did not wish to accept his sacrifice, but as Grand Master it is my duty."

I could not see the point of either of them being killed and asked him to explain if he could.

"What is the point of a soldier's death?" he asked.

"His society expects it of him."

"Yes. You have answered your own question. And now I will put one to you. Would you die for the sake of the Christian faith?"

"Probably."

"Yet you have little respect for the Church and its creed."

"Or for its rites."

"There you are wrong, for rites are a shadow of the truth. I summoned you to me by what is remembered as the Harp of Orpheus. You called up a Presence as mischievous and sweet as Meg by a rite far older. You had faith that you heard. I had faith that I saw. Reality? We are fools to ask what is reality when all we touch and see and are is empty space and energy. Within the Purpose there are rites named of earth and rites named of heaven all intermingled in all religions and culminating in that purest and simplest of rites: the Communion of the Christian with the Purpose."

"For you then what *is* the Purpose?" I asked.

"How often there is more beauty in living things than needed for survival! Consider the peacock's tail and the feathers of the bird of paradise! To attract a mate and be recognized, we are told, but that could be achieved by a fraction of the display. Consider the majestic antlers of

178

the stag! A magnificence and nothing but a handicap. The colors of the butterfly — they have a use, but not to that extent of glory. Consider the *Columns of the Sun* and your late *Holy Well!* What use to your survival or the survival of the race are those? They have only one conceivable value and that is to the observer. What the Purpose is we cannot know, but observation must be within it. Observe this garden of the earth and understand that when you cease to observe and to love you exist no more!"

"Then death is the end."

"You miss my meaning, Alfgif. I know nothing of death except that we should not whine for immortality. Take joy in the gift of life! If the object of my life is finished with my death, I rejoice that I have been able to serve. If it is not finished, I rejoice that there is still a use for me."

He said that was enough of preaching and remained silent. The scent of the earth was stronger than I had ever known it. Meg ran between us, caressing his face with her whiskers and then returning to my feet. I asked him to tell me about Paddy.

"Paddy was a healer of the animals. A Robin. His coven was formed of all his friends though few were conscious of it. He was simpler and more saintly and quicker than I. He would have seen that you could never have abused your gift as I believed you had. He said you had the makings of a leader."

"A shaman?"

"A Robin. I like that happy, English name. The healer. The provider of joy."

"And of sendings to the innocent," I added, remembering Odolaga.

"Forgive him! He acted from foolish fear, and you would not blame the beast which charges when it cannot run. And now for this girl of yours, my strange, chaste sorcerer! It seems you can copy the attack of the carnivore but not the tempest of its mating."

"How do you know?"

"Only a monk could have so much passion and remain celibate. Were you never married?"

"For two weeks."

"What happened?"

"She died in my arms."

"I see. Guilt. But that was not beyond psychiatrists."

"I'll have none of them. I am what I am and know more than they."

"But your tiger brother — couldn't he cure you?"

"No. He said that a white larva had made its home in my wretched organ and he could not conjure it to leave."

"I think you would not let him, Alfgif. You believed in your guilt and clung to it. But now will you let me? I can make you as a Robin of old days whose maidens would hang wreathes of poppies on the symbol of fertility. Will you be ashamed to dance naked with me?"

I might have been, but those gentle, piercing eyes would not release mine. And there was I naked while he, stripped to the waist only, like tiger brother, raised his arms in a hieratic gesture as if he were throwing over his shoulders the skin and tail of the God.

He began to beat the ground with his feet, always circling around me face to face, and I kept time with him. What ritual I was treading out I could not know, though there were memories of the forest and memories of the eager hunting dance which I had performed for my dinner but never for myself.

"Your horns are spread between sky and sky, my Alfgif. You have driven away your rivals and the herd of does awaits you. As a bird dances for its mate, so must you. Tell him, Valley, to dance for grandson Alfgif! Tell him, Meg, to dance with you! As we dance, so must you."

There was much more, but that is what I remember. He circled me, chanting, and each time he passed a young plant of broom he plucked a green twig from it like a browsing goat. In the trance of beating feet I was aware only of his hands and eyes; nor was I conscious of the erection, being so long forgotten, until he flung the wreath that he had been twisting as if it were a quoit over a peg.

He told me to dress and have no fear.

"Mate after mate is yours if you wish, and if you wish only for one she will never leave you. What is her name? I will call her."

"Rita. But she cannot receive. She would not hear you."

"Better so, Alfgif! In you she will find the future and in her you will find the past. Go now, and tomorrow be with her!"

"Shall I see you again?"

"As a passing friend it may be, with the simplicity of Paddy."

I asked him if he really lived on the Syrian shore as Paddy had told me.

"Often enough, because that is where all religions meet and all traditions remain. Among my ancestors were reigning devils, or Grand Masters if you wish. Jacques de Molay, Master of the Temple, burnt for heresy. Plantagenets reverenced by Christian and pagan alike and true to both. It may well be that you and I are not the first of our two families who have met and prayed together."

"Can I drive you anywhere?" I asked, the question sounding absurdly out of time and place. "How are you going?"

"As I came, Alfgif."

He shook hands, blessed me and was gone, vanishing with the skill of tiger brother and with only the rustle of his footsteps to show that he was most certainly passing through the trees and not above them.

## September 8

I write in Oxford the last entry of this notebook which started off as an attempt to cure induced dementia and carried on as the record of an expedition along the frontiers between illusion and reality. Since the journey is at an end, my travel diary stops like any other.

Meg and I went home and slept more peacefully than for weeks past. In the morning I walked down to Rita's cottage and found her packing up books and putting the place in order. I had not seen her for four days. She thought, she said, that I was too upset over the *Holy Well* to come and say good-bye. I explained that I had been busy in quite another way, not painting nor grieving but learning the responsibilities of a Robin.

She reproached me with being more sunk in myself than ever.

"And I can't understand how you look so well since you came back from Paris," she added.

"It wasn't Paris. It was essential that Concha Pirrone should not know where I was really going."

"Not to Izar Odolaga!"

"Close to him. But it's too confused a story for now."

"So little is for here and now except Meg."

I longed to tell her that she had never been out of the here and now and never would be, but it was not a moment to choose when she was rightly annoyed with me.

"I came to ask you if you would picnic on the downs with me this evening. It will be another warm night."

"No, Alfgif, I can't. I shall be busy packing."

"Once you asked me if I would start a coven and dance with you in the moonlight."

"And you said you were no good at dancing."

"Because my tail was still at the tailors. A white cloth, bread, wine and meat, the Robin used to bring. And oysters arrived in Penminster this morning. Shall we walk up the valley from my house or would you prefer a broomstick?"

"I will imagine the broomstick."

"Then you will come?"

"Of course I'll come."

At sunset we walked across the bullock paradise and up the smooth breast of the downs. She was talking with forced gaiety and I felt that she regretted her decision, believing that it would only lead to another memory of the door between us which would not open. As for myself, swinging one of Ginny's great baskets and with Meg in my pocket, I was often looking away into the even dusk like an animal bound across country for its mate and nervous of interruption, though I could not have said by whom or by what. I seemed to sense that we were accompanied, perhaps by the blessing of Julian Molay seeking us from wherever he stabled his stallion and comforted some other secret disciple, perhaps by that which had been present the night before and was flitting along with us to look down on its home.

Rita noticed my quick glances and asked suddenly: "There isn't anyone else coming?"

"Not unless Meg has invited a guest."

"Shouldn't there be thirteen in all?"

"That's only on high holidays."

The valley was silver, as on that night when I met my vixen and was overcome by terror. The stream had widened into a lake of haze stationary between the woodland and the oaks. We were above it on the short and windless grass, which still held the heat of the afternoon. A Robin of old days could not have appointed a better rendezvous for his coven, since there was no path for the wanderer, and the mist, down in Penminster and the valley, would have kept the cottagers at home.

I laid out the white cloth in a dry combe below the ridge and spread out the food and drink for the Maiden of the Coven. The moon turned to white the pale gold of her forearms and the wine in the glasses. Her gaiety, true or false, did not return. We might have been picnicking on a cloud, like putti above the solemnity of an Italian betrothal, reverent but with growing cheerfulness as the nectar was handed around.

When our moonlit supper was over we were at ease as in the first days of friendship, and she was finding in this peace either comfort or resignation. She lay with her hands behind her head. The irregular rise and fall of her breasts told me that her thoughts were troubled by so much perfection which was still imperfect, and that she was near sobbing.

A moment of difficulty. I could not cross the barrier of white tablecloth, breaking our old relationship so unexpectedly that she might mistrust the truth of the new, nor could I remind her abruptly that she had come to dance with me. It was Meg who saved me. I said to myself that, by God, if I had any power over Meg I should use it now! In the ears of my mind was the summons which Molay had sent across the valley, calling it the Harp of Orpheus, and I now found in it a rhythm which I stroked and

184

tapped out imperceptibly on Meg's fur. She dived from my pocket, stood on hind legs to inquire, then tumbled, rolled and twisted into that waltz when one could swear she had an unseen partner.

Rita sat up to watch her, and at last I could say: "Come then! You too!"

It started with the birdlike flappings and posturings of modern dance and then turned into a more formal minuet in which we pirouetted under arched hands, separated, and in fun bowed and curtsied.

"But you are dancing as if there were music!" she exclaimed.

Yes, I was, for rhythm remembered was clearer than ever.

"The minstrel has come with Master Robin," I replied and speeded up the time.

Side by side we improvised the steps, never failing each other, sometimes with both hands joined, sometimes with my arm around her waist.

Now whether it was deliberate or whether, as she insisted later, she had tripped over the excited Meg I shall never know, but we came down on the turf together. Then the only dancing was of lips and arms and flung garments caught on the mats of the thyme, and there was no doubt at all that Molay, the Devil, could heal with the power of a saint.

"And all that time you wanted me so much?" she asked.

"All the time."

"But I told you over and over again."

"I was afraid I should disappoint you."

"But how could you, my love?"

The truth was for me only, so I answered that she had been right when she said I was so seldom here and now.

"I would not expect a Robin to be anything else. Robin — that will be my name for you always."

"And you must really leave the cottage tomorrow?"

"I thought forever," she said. "But now you must come with me and be very near me for a day or two and bring me home again to all your family that I shall never see."